8:17 PM, RUE DARLING

ESSENTIAL TRANSLATIONS SERIES 17

**Canada Council
for the Arts**

**Conseil des Arts
du Canada**

Guernica Editions Inc. acknowledges the support of
the Canada Council for the Arts and the Ontario Arts Council.
The Ontario Arts Council is an agency of the Government of Ontario.
We acknowledge the financial support of the Government of Canada through the
National Translation Program for Book Publishing for our translation activities.
We also acknowledge the financial support of the Government of Canada
through the Canada Book Fund (CBF) for our publishing activities.

**ONTARIO ARTS COUNCIL
CONSEIL DES ARTS DE L'ONTARIO**

50 YEARS OF ONTARIO GOVERNMENT SUPPORT OF THE ARTS

50 ANS DE SOUTIEN DU GOUVERNEMENT DE L'ONTARIO AUX ARTS

Bernard Émond

8:17 PM,
RUE
DARLING

Translated from the French by John Gilmore

GUERNICA

TORONTO – BUFFALO – LANCASTER (U.K.)
2014

Michael Mirolla, editor
Guernica Editions Inc.
P.O. Box 76080, Abbey Market, Oakville, (ON), Canada L6M 3H5
2250 Military Road, Tonawanda, N.Y. 14150-6000 U.S.A.

Distributors:
University of Toronto Press Distribution,
5201 Dufferin Street, Toronto (ON), Canada M3H 5T8
Gazelle Book Services, White Cross Mills, High Town, Lancaster LA1 4XS U.K.

First edition.
Printed in Canada.

Legal Deposit – First Quarter
Library of Congress Catalog Card Number: 2013953836
Library and Archives Canada Cataloguing in Publication

Émond, Bernard, 1951-
[20 h 17, rue Darling. English]
8:17 pm, rue Darling / Bernard Émond ; John Gilmore, translator.

(Essential translations series ; 17)
Translation of: 20 h 17, rue Darling.
Issued in print and electronic formats.
ISBN 978-1-55071-846-1 (pbk.).--ISBN 978-1-55071-847-8 (epub).--
ISBN 978-1-55071-848-5 (mobi)

I. Gilmore, John, 1951-, translator II. Title. III. Title: 8:17
pm, rue Darling. IV. Title: 20 h 17, rue Darling. English. V. Series: Essential
translations series ; 17

PS8559.M62V5613 2014   C843'.6   C2013-907542-9
                                                C2013-907543-7

My name is Gérard and I'm an alcoholic. I've been sober for two months and two days. I'm sitting in a motel room beside the Atlantic. I'm looking at the ocean. I don't like the ocean, but I'm looking at it anyway. My mind is all over the place. I'm thinking about luck and fate, and things like that. It's December. The view is boring, just snow falling on dark, dreary waves. I really shouldn't be here. But I am.

◆

It all began seven months ago in a hotel room in Montreal, at the corner of Guy and René-Lévesque.

The first thing I saw when I walked in was the mini-bar. I thanked God they hadn't given me the key. Not that that stopped me. I still tried to open it. I was thirsty.

I know all about thirsty. I've spent my whole life thirsty.

The beautiful thing about booze is that for a few hours or a few days life is simple. All your failures, your faults, and your mistakes; all your needs, your worries, and your discontents; all the hurt you've caused – everything is reduced to a single problem: finding the next drink. It's a great way to consolidate your debts. Life is complicated, drinking is simple.

Though obviously there's the morning after. Or the week after, or the month after. The day when you sober up. The day the bill comes due.

The mini-bar was locked good. Lots of times before I'd lost everything, but this was the first time I'd lost everything sober. Believe me, there's a difference.

It's true, I lost everything that night, though to be honest I didn't really have much left to lose. I'd already lost my wives, my children, my homes, my jobs, my friends, my dignity, and all my retirement savings. I'd even lost a dog, a beautiful Lab. I don't know what happened to him, the poor guy; I lost my car and he was in it. This time all I lost was an old bed, a rickety table, a worn-out armchair, and a second-hand fridge and stove. And a few clothes. And Zola's *Les Rougon-Macquart*. In hardcover, the Pléiade edition. All five volumes. My only real loss.

We hold on to whatever we can. For me, it's having a routine. I'm as methodical sober as I was when I was into the booze (nothing but Cutty Sark for me, straight, no ice, no water, no more than three before lunch, except on a binge). So in that hotel room I did what I'd done every night at home for the past seven months: I forced myself to watch the TV news. I switched it off after the sports. I brushed my teeth (with the little Red Cross kit the fireman gave me). I emptied my pockets and folded my clothes neatly. Then I went to bed and read. Usually I read Zola before turning out the light. But that night there was only the hotel Bible. I don't remember what passage it was. I don't even remember finishing the page. I must have fallen asleep like a rock. I was a wreck.

◆

The next morning it really hit me. I woke up at six in the dark. I got out of bed to go for a piss and it was while sitting on the toilet (I always sit down in the morning) that it hit me like a ton of bricks. Why me? I don't mean: "Why did God pick my building to blow up?" Or: "What did I do to deserve this?" I'm not that kind of guy. When tragedy strikes, I don't ask why. Tragedy strikes because that's life and we all have to die some time. Tragedy is all around us, it's the bread we eat and the air we breathe. The only thing to do when tragedy strikes is to say to yourself: OK, here we go again. God give me the strength to get through the day. God take away my thirst.

I'm not a believer but I try hard.

No, what I mean is, Why *me*? Why was *I* alive that morning, sitting on the toilet pissing? Why did *I* survive? With my routines, I should have been dead. At 8:17 pm every night I'm sitting in my armchair listening to the concert on FM – well, either the concert or the *fifi* announcer yakking on about it. When you can't afford concert tickets or CDs you listen to a lot of radio. The yakking comes with the territory, like black flies in the woods in June. And I'm willing to put up with a lot to hear Beethoven's third violin sonata, or something that good.

So, in the normal course of things, I should have been dead. If I was still alive, it was because of a shoelace that came undone, a Chinese guy who ran a stop sign, the first of my three ex-wives, and Step Nine of Alcoholic's Anonymous (if you're not a member, it goes like this: *We have made amends directly to everyone we have harmed, wherever possible, except when doing so would injure them or others.*)

There's an old musician's joke. A tourist is lost in Montreal. He sees an old man carrying a violin case under his arm and asks him how to get to Place des Arts. The violinist replies: "Practice, practice, practice." Well, I believe in practice. I have a hard time with the

Twelve Steps, especially the ones about the Greater Power (and that's six out of twelve). But I practice them all, as best I can. I'm like a priest who's lost his faith and who tries to get it back by reciting the mass with more fervour than he ever did. I've got to the point where I'd believe in Santa Claus if it would help me stay sober. So I practice, practice, practice. And when Chantal (the first of my three ex-wives) called me, for the third time that month, I didn't have a choice. Like they say, I had to make amends.

I have to smile whenever I go over to Chantal's place, a triplex on Esplanade that we bought for a song in the sixties (and that I kept paying for, long after the divorce). I'd just started at the *Journal de Montreal*, we were in love, and we thought it would be cool to live facing the mountain on a street full of hippies. Now the yuppies have taken over the neighbourhood, adding a zero on the end of the house prices, and Chantal is sitting on a cool million, damn her. Chantal, Chantal, Chantal. She came from an Outremont family and she liked the idea of marrying an east-end bum turned poet and tabloid journalist. She used to love it at breakfast. I'd tell her about the gory murders from the night before, the arsons, the cars flattened like pancakes. Then off she'd go to university to play counsellor. The students used to call her *Madame Bjiiir* because she talked with a stuck-up Parisian accent and puckered her lips like a chicken's ass whenever she said *bonjour*. I used to bug her about it, too. She made me pay; it was only fair, I guess. And I'm still paying, out of habit. And maybe because I like it.

We're not getting any younger, Chantal and I. We're both almost sixty. She has her aches and pains like the rest of us, and now that I'm sober she calls me up from time to time, asking me to do odd jobs for her around the house. Like she can't afford a plumber or a carpenter, the bitch. But, fair enough, you don't call a plumber to change a washer. So I do it, while she stands around reminding me how I've wasted my life; how the three poems I published in *Liberté* when I was twenty are worth more than all the stories I wrote for the *Journal* over the next forty years; and how much I've disappointed her for one thing or another – because of the child I never gave her (and the ones I've given other women – she never forgave me for those), because of the books I didn't write, the women I ran around with when we were married, and all the forty-ouncers of Scotch I drank (according to my calculations, more than ten thousand bottles in forty years, which is about ten cubic metres of good Scotch whiskey, enough to half-fill one of those above-ground swimming pools that people have in their back yards).

Divorce is like marriage, it takes time to mature. After thirty years I think Chantal and I have finally made a success of our divorce. She's got a great sense of humour, she's as sharp as a tack and a good judge of character. If only she wasn't such an unbearable snob. I don't know what she sees in me, a hard-core alcoholic, rough-around-the-edges, gone back to live in poverty in the disaster of a neighbourhood I grew up in. I guess we're like family now, Chantal and I. She's pulled me out of a hole more than once, bless her, even after I walked out on her. And now I owe her one, again. Because if she hadn't called me over that night, I would have died listening to Beethoven. Or (just my luck) the *fifi* announcer.

I don't know how to say thank you in Cantonese, but I guess I should learn. It all happened so fast: I left Chantal's, I got in my car, I pulled away, and I was hit by a Chinese guy running a stop sign. For once I meet a Chinese guy doing more than thirty and it has to be some absent-minded businessman in a BMW whipping right along without looking where he's going (though, who knows, maybe he was fresh off the boat and couldn't read traffic signs from left to right). I don't know if you've ever tried filling out a joint accident report form with someone who can't speak French or English. It's no walk in the park. We ended up having to call the police. They

7

were young officers. I didn't know them, and I can tell you they weren't very happy about being called out for a couple of bent fenders and an immigrant investor. (Obviously, I didn't count: when you look the way I do and you're driving a Pinto from the days of the October Crisis, believe me, you don't count, in the eyes of the police or anyone else). But the fact remains, the Chinese guy also saved my life. The accident happened at 7:45 and we stayed there for a good hour chewing the rag in Cantonese. My building blew up at 8:17, according to the clock the firemen found in the rubble. If it wasn't for the car accident I would have had plenty of time to get back to my armchair, my radio, and my fate. We don't amount to much, do we?

But the worst thing was the shoelace. That's what really saved me. The shoelace that came undone. It only took me thirty seconds to tie it at the bottom of Chantal's stairs – just long enough to get in the way of the Son of Heaven in his BMW.

There's something deeply humiliating about owing your life to a shoelace.

◆

My name is Gérard and I'm an alcoholic. My name is Gérard and I'm an alcoholic.

I repeat my mantra in front of the bathroom mirror every morning, I do my little Antoine Doinel number so I don't forget who I am. But in the hotel room that morning I have to admit I was having my doubts. I was a man who was alive because his shoelace had come undone. It's like saying I owed my life to a gust of wind or a fluke accident. Or nothing at all. Frankly, I couldn't bear the thought.

"We made a decision to turn our will and our lives over to the care of God as we understood Him." AA, Step Three. Admitting that a Greater Power exists. Accepting that He's watching over every hair on every newborn baby in every parish on the planet. If you buy that, then with a little effort of Faith you can probably find some meaning in life (as long as you can convince yourself that famine, torture, and Céline Dion are part of the Divine Plan). If you don't buy it, then you have to admit that God doesn't care about us any more than we care about the grains of sand we trample on at the beach. In that case, I don't see why I shouldn't immediately start drinking the other half of my swimming pool full of Scotch.

Except I don't want to die.

Not right away, anyway. And not from booze. Not in a pool of puke and diarrhoea. Not in the street. I want to die in a bed with clean sheets and I want two or three people to remember me as a man. That's all, just a man.

So life has to have a meaning. And my shoelace has to be part of the Divine Plan.

At that point, the unshaven bastard in the mirror says:

– You're even crazier sober than you are drunk, Gerry.

To which I reply:

– No shit.

OK, fine, there doesn't have to be a Divine Plan. But something has to make sense. So why me? Why me, three-times divorced, a father cursed by his kids, a liar, a cheater, a thief, a man who for forty years has worshipped only one thing – the little ship on the yellow label on a bottle of Cutty Sark? Why was I spared when my neighbours died? Do their deaths have any meaning? Did baby Jesus have something in mind when he snuffed out a little old lady who never hurt a soul? And a three-year-old kid? Why them, and not me?

◆

All my life I've covered fires, accidents, crimes, and disasters. Tragedy was my stock in trade. Even now, in my forced retirement, I have to stop myself from chasing sirens in the hope of finding survivors and witnesses to interview, a horrific scene to describe, or a depressing detail to spice up the story. I was a hack reporter for the local rag. I covered the police beat for thirty-odd years. There's nothing I haven't seen. Bodies cut in half. Faces kicked to a pulp. I saw the corpse of a baby so charred it looked like burnt pork roast. Once I saw a guy pour gasoline over himself then light a cigarette, while a bunch of us journalists and cameramen just stood around watching, waiting for him to do it. Once I counted eleven stretchers being carried out of a shopping centre, after some nut case went berserk with a gun. And then I went right in, right after – for the benefit of my readers, you understand. I had to tell them about the puddles of blood.

There's not much I haven't seen, in living colour.

You become indifferent. You have to. You can't go puke behind the ambulance every time you see human porridge. If you can't take it, you'd better change jobs. The problem is, the more indifferent you become, the more you lose respect for suffering. I'll admit it, I lost it. I don't know if I started drinking because I lost respect for suffering, or if I lost respect for suffering because I started drinking. In the end I guess it doesn't really matter. What I do know is that one morning I woke up in hospital with four broken teeth, cracked ribs, and testicles as big as grapefruit. They told me I'd followed a man who had just lost his daughter in a fire. They told me I kept pestering him with questions. They told me he went berserk and it took three policemen to stop him from kicking me to death. I only remember because they told me. I was too out of it that night to remember anything.

Maudite booze.

When I got to my street it was all blocked off. There must have been twenty emergency vehicles, lights flashing like it was Christmas. I got out of my heap and walked over to the police car that was blocking the way. The cop behind the wheel was a veteran. He recognized me right away.

– Hey, Gerry! Don't tell me you're back at the *Journal!*

Talk about being famous. I stuck out like Barabbas at the Passion. But I didn't feel like telling him the story of my life. I just said:

– Nope. I live here.

– *Ah, oui?* What number?

– 2068.

– Tough luck, Gerry boy. You won't be sleeping in your own bed tonight.

As explosions go, I'd seen worse. The buildings on either side of mine were still standing, but mine was a mountain of rubble. All five apartments had collapsed on top of one another. Only the back wall was still there. You could see pieces of the three floors still attached to it. Amazingly, there was a wardrobe, too, stuck to the back wall, hanging in mid-air, with clothes still on the hangers. It was the kind of image TV audiences loved. The moles from

Station 20 were already at work, digging down into the rubble, looking for victims. Or bodies.

It didn't seem real. It was like it was happening to someone else. All my old instincts kicked into play. I made a mental note of the number of emergency vehicles, calculated how many firemen were on the scene, looked around me for sobbing survivors or excited witnesses. But there was just the usual crowd of onlookers. So I headed for the fire department's mobile command post that was parked nearby. I had to pass a canteen truck, where a few firemen were gathered. Someone called out:

– Hey, Gerry! Don't tell me they took you back at the *Journal!*

I gave them a wave but didn't say a word. I stepped into the mobile command post. Gros Morin and Big Bélanger were slouched in front of their radios and computer screens. Lieutenant Panaccio was eating a sandwich. It was pretty calm, the rush was over.

– Hey, Gerry! they erupted.

To cut them short, I told them that I wasn't back at the *Journal,* that I was one of the tenants in the building that had just collapsed, and that the guys from Station 20 weren't going to find my body in the rubble.

They asked me about the other occupants and I told them what I knew. Then I got the latest from them. The moles hadn't found any survivors or bodies yet, and there probably wouldn't be anything definite before morning. They didn't know how many people were in the building, but there were at least three – the wife and little girl of a man who walked out of the place just before it blew up, and a little old lady who was always home. My downstairs neighbours ... the old lady on the first floor ... it still wasn't sinking in. I asked about the cause of the explosion. They didn't have a clue. Gros Morin raised his arms:

– Act of God, Gerry boy. Act of God.

I said goodnight and headed over to the red school bus, the one the fire department uses to provide shelter for victims at the scene. The 1400, the firemen call it, the disaster victim's bus. I knew there I could at least stay warm, there'd be coffee, and the volunteers from Sun Youth would give me a tooth brush, a shaving kit, and a voucher for three nights at a hotel, no charge.

There's nothing quite like tragedy to clear a space around you. It's worse than bad breath. At the front of the bus, the atmosphere was like a holiday camp. The neighbours, the ones who hadn't lost anything but who were put on the bus in case of another explosion, were yakking away like school kids on a fire drill. At the back of the bus, far from the others, there was a man staring at his feet.

He was in his thirties. He had a beard and an ear ring and he was built like a brick shithouse, the kind of guy you wouldn't want to run into in a dark alley. My downstairs neighbour. I'd passed him a few times on the stairs but I didn't know his name. I'd never liked him, partly because of his music (if you can call it that). It was always too loud and I could hear it through the floor. But mostly because of the insults he shouted at his woman and kids at all hours of the day and night. I had to listen to that, too. Now here he was, slumped in the back seat of the bus, white as a ghost, in a kind of stupor. The bruiser had turned to melting butter. He was a broken man, a knot of pure pain. It's hard to imagine that brutes like him have feelings, so when you see them suffering it really hits you. I kept my distance, just like the neighbours. I sat down as far from him and the others as I could. And I started thinking about my Zolas, the only thing I'd miss. I know, it wasn't very noble of me, but that's the way it is. People are selfish bastards.

A couple of minutes later a teenager got on the bus, a big slouch of a kid, stoned out of his mind. Darvon or Empracet was my guess. The son of the guy with the beard. He stumbled down the aisle, pie-eyed, looking like he'd just discovered America.

– *Tabarnak*, pa, the place is gone!

His father didn't move a muscle. He didn't even look up. He just sat there, staring at his feet. And then the bus started moving, off to deliver its cargo of disaster victims to hotels around the city.

◆

When you get right down to it, it was Gros Morin's fault. Act of God, he told me in the mobile command post. I know, it's just one of those things you say, but it's the wrong thing to say to an alcoholic anonymous who's having a hard time coming to terms with the Power greater than himself. OK, Gros Morin couldn't have known. But the damage was done anyway.

I have a lot of respect for the Red Cross. Sure, there was that little problem with HIV, but that doesn't stop me remembering all the good things they do in the world, for refugees, disaster victims, and other stray dogs without a collar. I've only got one gripe with the Red Cross: do they have to put scented shaving cream in the toilet kits they hand out to victims? My first day homeless and I was going to walk around smelling like a hooker.

Act of God. I admit, it's got a nice ring to it. And it does lend itself to reflection, even if it is an English expression. But what did God-as-we-understand-Him-to-be really have in mind when he killed at least three innocent people and saved a loser like me? That's what I wanted to know at 6:30 in the morning, smelling like cinnamon, putting on the same clothes I took off the night before, in a hotel room so bland Plato could have used it as an archetype. They were all innocent, as far as I knew. For the seven months I lived there I can't exactly say I had a wild social life. But I said hello a few times to the old lady on her balcony on the first floor. She was almost blind, I think. What terrible thing had she done in her darkened world to warrant dying like that? And what about the wife and daughter of the guy with the beard? I hardly ever saw them, but it wasn't hard to imagine what they'd had to endure living with that hulk of an alpha male. So, what? The Good Lord has started taking it out on the little guys? He gets his rocks off kicking people when they're down?

There is no Good Lord.

My thirst was back. I needed a drink. There's nothing quite like a double Scotch on an empty stomach to lighten the load of existence. It's almost instant. Even when you puke it up there's usually enough time for a little alcohol to get to the brain. God, I could taste it. The mini-bar was still locked. I swear, if there'd been a tool box in the room I would have demolished that lock and my sobriety with three bangs on a cold chisel. But there wasn't. So I went looking for coffee instead. I was desperate.

If cirrhosis of the liver is the disease of alcoholics, stomach ulcers are the occupational hazard of alcoholics on the wagon, thanks to the industrial quantities of bad coffee we imbibe at AA meetings and every time the craving for booze hits us. And it hits often. The hotel restaurant was closed. I thought about strangling the manager who'd decided to tweak his profit margin by opening the restaurant at 7:00 rather than 6:30. Then I left. The night before, I hadn't given any thought to the neighbourhood I'd been dropped off in. I could have driven my car to the hotel instead of riding the bus. But there are times we all need to be mothered, even if it is by a surly fireman in his fifties who's winding down his career driving victims around town in a little red school bus.

I had a vile cup of coffee in a greasy spoon on Sainte-Catherine, then started walking east. The class war is for real, and anyone who tells you it's not is a liar: may their nose grow, their Quebec Liberal Party card spontaneously burst into flames, and their cell phone give them cancer. It's a war waged by the rich on everyone else. On one side of town you've got the two million dollar sugar shacks in Westmount; on the other side, the hovels of Hochelaga-Maisonneuve. And for some people, it's just the street. Walk down Sainte-Catherine from west to east if you want a crash course in political economy. It should be a required assignment for all the arrogant little shits polishing the seat of their pants at the Hautes études commerciales. Walking down Sainte-Catherine might not change their thinking, but at least they'd see how the rest of humanity has to live so they can eat *canard à la lime* and drink Pouilly-Fuissé.

At seven o'clock in the morning, in the shadows of the bank and trust company towers, the homeless crawl out of their holes to start the day while the prostitutes are finishing theirs. Meanwhile, in the leafy residential neighbourhoods, aggressive young junior executives wake up under their Linen Chest duvets while secretaries put on their faces in front of their bathroom mirrors. The anglo riff-raff on the West Island read *The Gazette* while the sheep in Laval and the other north-shore 'burbs flip through *La Presse*, make their shopping lists, and head to the mall in their Voyager minivans with the remote starters. But on rue Sainte-Catherine, the down-and-out are already out, in full view of the world. Misery drags it heels. Misery looks for a hit. Misery sells its ass.

If you take rue Ontario east and go through the tunnel on Moreau, you get to Hochelaga-Maisonneuve. It's home. *Chez nous.* The third poorest neighbourhood in the best country in the world. Here, misery isn't just on the street, it's in the home. Not all of them, mind you, but most. When I was young everyone had a job. We were poor but we had our dignity, as they say, and the kids were well looked after. My father and my uncles worked up the hill at the Angus rail shops. They had good steady jobs with decent pay. The guys who worked there were like the aristocrats of the neighbourhood. But there were lots of other places to work, too – the foundries, the garment factories, Viau Biscuits, the sugar refinery, the port. My uncle Jos used to keep a rowboat moored at the foot of rue Dézéry. He'd row out into the river, tie up to the Jacques Cartier Bridge, and go fishing out there, can you imagine? Today, the Angus shops are closed, people with any kind of job are in the minority, dignity has left town, and the teenagers carry knives. Not all of them, but a lot of them.

That's my *chez nous*. I grew up on rue Lafontaine between Aylwin and Cuvillier, in a big ground-floor apartment in a building made of yellow-glazed bricks. The vacant lot next door became our yard. My father planted a plum tree in that yard. It's still there. It died recently but the guy who owns the lot hasn't cut it down yet. So it just stands there, dried up, at the bottom of the hill that we used to slide down in winter on pieces of cardboard.

I lived all over the city before moving back to my old neighbourhood, to rue Darling, two hundred feet from our old plum tree. I lived in Outremont, NDG,

Mile End, and the Plateau. I lived in Old Montreal and Villeray. I've had apartments that cost fifteen hundred a month and I've had roach hotels. I've lived in chrome-plated condos and in one of those yuppy rabbit hutches in a high-rise downtown. I even had a bungalow out in Brossard (big mistake, like everything else about my third marriage). But I can tell you now, there's nothing like a four-and-a-half unheated in the old neighbourhood. It's not my fault I'm from down here. I don't know what I was looking for in those other places, but I know I didn't find it. Cutty Sark tastes the same everywhere, but it wasn't until I got back to Hochelaga that I started tasting water again. I hit rock bottom. I lost everything I had, but I found sobriety again in my old neighbourhood. Amen and Praise the Lord, as they say in Little Burgundy.

There wasn't much left of my unheated four-and-a-half on the third floor on Darling, just the calendar with the Chinese pin-up girl that the previous tenant had left hanging on the back wall of the kitchen. I left it there, maybe as a reminder that the world is vast and women are beautiful. The rest of my worldly belongings were now compacted under a mountain of rubble. I patted myself on the back for my wisdom in buying the Pléiades edition on Bible paper, made to last 300 years. Lieutenant Geoffrion was just climbing out of the rubble when

2 1

I arrived. Gaston Geoffrion, but they call him Boom Boom after his idol, number 5 on the Canadiens back in the fifties. The lieutenant is a short man with an eagle eye that he's developed from years of investigating fires. He once spent weeks in a burnt-out church, going through the rubble with a tooth brush. He found the cause. He always finds the cause. You just have to be methodical and persistent, and Boom Boom is both. He was so absorbed in his thoughts that he didn't see me approaching.

– Christ, you scared me! Where the hell'd you come from? *Écoute*, Gerry, I can't tell you a thing. Not yet.

– Was it arson?

– No, *je pense pas*. If it was, the guys from the cop shop would be down here, messing things up.

What the Boomer meant was that when you're investigating a fire you have to be very careful not to accidentally destroy the evidence you're looking for. He doesn't trust anyone, least of all the police.

– You've got no idea? Gas? The furnace? Somebody storing dangerous products?

– No. The explosion was really ... strange.

– Strange?

– *Écoute*, Gerry. The more time I spend talking, the less time I spend thinking. And I've got to think. You want details, call Lieutenant Giguère at Public Affairs. *Salut*.

– Wait! Wait! *Attends!* At least tell me how many victims there were.

– Six. I think that's all they found.

– Six? You sure?

He was already gone, nose buried in his sketches, lost in his train of thought.

Six. As far as I knew, there were eight of us living there. The bearded guy and his son were on the bus. So, either there'd been visitors in the building the night it blew up, or I was dead and I didn't know it yet. Time for another coffee.

◆

Good bartenders are the guardian angels of alcoholics. If I'm alive, it's because someone treated me like a man when I was almost an animal. I miss bartenders. It's things like that that make me thirsty sometimes. The lost fraternity of the bar. But we make do with what we've got, and what I've got now is the Bien Bon. The Bien Bon is a snack-bar at the corner of Ontario and Darling. It's twelve stools along a counter, it's open six days a week from five am to five pm, and it serves the best shepherd's pie in the city. I have lunch there every day except Sunday, and I often eat breakfast there, too, especially those mornings when I wake up thinking too much about the little ship. The walls used to be pink, but now they're covered with newspaper clippings, pictures of baby animals, naughty cartoons, cheerful maxims, and magazine photos of TV stars and cars (all of them Fords, I always wondered why). Rose, the owner and cook, has a thing for Willie Lamothe and the back wall of the place is like a shrine, covered with photos of the country singer from Saint-Hyacinthe at every stage of his career. Angéla, the waitress, is tall, with jet-black hair. She's in her forties and perfect: she says *bonjour* with a trace of an Acadian accent, she serves me without any small talk, and she leaves me alone.

That morning, everyone at the Bien Bon was talking about the explosion on Darling. I resisted the temptation to brag about my close encounter with death. I don't know how many times I've seen people bring their lawn chairs out front so they can sit comfortably while watching their neighbour's house burn down. Behind the phony compassion of people who chirp "Poor you!" there's the curiosity of the scavenger. But who am I judge? For 30 years I earned my living furnishing carrion to the vultures. At the Bien Bon, I just wanted to be left alone. Besides, I had to make a list. There are two kinds of people in the world: those who make lists and those who don't. Obviously, I belong to the first group. And starting over from scratch is no small potatoes, as my mother used to say. So I took out my notebook (some people carry a Swiss Army knife, I carry a notebook, tool of my trade). And I started my list:

1. Bank machine.
2. Buy – a real razor, a real toothbrush, unscented shaving cream.
3. Buy – socks and underwear.
4. Buy – second-hand clothes and a suitcase at the Glaneuses or Value Village.

I was just getting to number five (go back to the hotel and change my clothes) when a young woman ran into the Bien Bon and threw herself at the pay phone. It took her three tries to get the number right. Her back was turned, but I could hear her hyperventilating. She was in a panic. She wasn't from around here, I could have sworn to that. She was wearing what all the women her age were wearing – tight jeans, a belly button, and something on top – but everything about her said she came from money. There was no answer at the other end of the line. She slammed the receiver down, then quickly picked it up and dialled again. I couldn't help listening. At the Bien Bon, the phone is on the wall right behind the stools. If you want privacy, go somewhere else.

– Monsieur Demers, *s'il vous plaît.* It's his daughter ... it's urgent ... *Oui,* I'll hold.

She turned around and leaned against the wall. It was my neighbour from the second floor, a student, a beautiful girl. I always wondered what she was doing down here. I had my theory. The English have a word for it: slumming. It's what the young bourgeois kids do: live with the peasants in the poor neighbourhoods for a while, to piss off their parents.

– Papa? *Écoute* Papa, I'm trying to reach Mama ... She's not home? ... You sure? ... I don't know ... *Non, non,* it's nothing ... nothing serious. Everything's fine ... *Écoute* Papa, I've gotta go. Talk to you later.

She hung up – and collapsed in a dead faint.

I don't remember exactly what happened next, but the end result was I got drawn into a story that was none of my business. She came to, thanks to Angéla's good care. I introduced myself as her neighbour and companion in misfortune. She recognized me. She asked if there had been any fatalities and if I knew any names. All I could get out of her was that she'd just come back from a trip, she'd lent her apartment to a friend, and she was worried. Very worried. I made a few calls on her behalf, to the fire department and the police station, and the next thing I knew we were in my car heading for the morgue. Angéla insisted on coming along, bless her. Nobody said much on the way. Angéla murmured a few reassuring words from the back seat while the girl sat up front, trembling like a leaf. Her name was Hélène.

There's nothing like a visit to the morgue to trigger a good existential crisis. At the end of the day, let's face it, it's the fridge for everyone. There's no escaping it. Some people get off on knowing there's at least one thing the rich can't buy their way out of, and that we're all equal in the drawers of the morgue. I think that way, too, sometimes. The trouble is, by the time you get there, you're in no state to enjoy your new-found equality.

It's funny how our screw-ups follow us around. The guy in charge of identifying bodies at the morgue recognized me. He didn't like me very much. You might say he was conscientious about guarding the privacy of his dead. We didn't even get to the hellos.

– Hey, asshole, I thought I told you I never wanted to see your face in here again. If you've got any questions, call the coroner's office. I don't talk to reporters.

The girl looked at me like I had the plague. I can't say I blame her. The guy in charge backed off a little when I told him we lived in the building that blew up on Darling. But the damage was done. Hélène turned cool towards me and insisted on going in alone for the ID. The guy in charge told Angéla and I to wait. We sat down on a vinyl-covered bench.

Angéla had been serving me every day for months but we'd never said more than a hundred words to each other. It was Angéla who spoke first:

– So. You're a journalist.

– Nope. Not any more.

Silence. I talk about my life at AA meetings, nowhere else. But, well, OK, she'd never done anything to hurt me, so, just to be polite, I added:

– I'm retired.

She looked at me, carefully. I could almost hear the wheels turning in her head. To put it mildly, I didn't fit the image of a retired journalist. I looked barely a rung up from the rubbies on Place d'Armes. I wasn't exactly the guy they were going to come looking for in my chic little Outremont pad when they needed someone to host election night coverage on TV. Angéla continued observing me. I braced myself for another nosy question, but after a moment she said:

– If there was someone in her apartment, it wasn't a friend. It was her mother.

– I know. I heard what she said on the phone, too.

– Why'd she lie?

– I don't know.

More silence. The guy in charge returned, alone. I asked him if the young woman had recognized anyone.

– I'm not allowed to say.

– Where is she?

– Gone.

Angéla and I looked at each other.

– Alone? I asked.

He made a face as if to say: "Of course, idiot!" As if I thought a corpse was going to walk out with her. Then he led me to a cubicle. It was my turn to look through photos of the victims.

What can you say about a corpse? Not much, as far as I'm concerned. In my line of work, I counted them, nothing more. In a pinch, when it wasn't too far-fetched, I might write "horribly mutilated" or "burnt to a crisp." My talent was describing how the corpse got to be a corpse, how the crime or accident or disaster happened. But the corpse itself? A person is born, grows up, falls in love, has children, reads books or spends his life sitting in front of the TV, fulfils his quota of nastiness or good deeds, and is either happy, miserable, or a bit of both. There's nothing much more to say when you see his corpse. What's lying there could be the body of a saint or a murderer, a Nobel Prize winner or a real estate developer, and it wouldn't make any difference. Whatever was beautiful or ugly in the person, sublime or ridiculous, is gone without a trace. There's only meat left. But that didn't help when I picked up the photos. They weren't the first stiffs I'd seen, but they shook me up. I was moved. Maybe because they were my neighbours and I'd known them (a little) when they were alive. Maybe because it could have been me. Or maybe because they were just innocent people, dead for no apparent reason. Mind you, whether you die for a reason or die for no reason, it doesn't make any difference when you're the one who's dead.

The first three weren't too much of a mess and I had no trouble recognizing them. There was the little old lady on the first floor, and the wife and daughter of the guy with the beard. I didn't know their family names and the guy in charge wasn't going to tell me. But seeing those photos really hit me, especially the little girl. Josée. The only name I knew. She was three years old. She used to say *bonjour* to me sometimes, from her window or the balcony, when I climbed the stairs. She was the only neighbour I'd actually talked to. A beautiful blonde girl. Her mother used to dress her up like a princess in clothes from the K-Mart. And now: nothing, a tiny thing, pale as a ghost, with plaster dust in her hair. I'm not the kind who goes gaga over children. To me they're just trained seals, as dumb as their parents, future consumers of soap operas, talk shows, and Kentucky Fried Chicken, dull civil servants in the making. A few escape that fate and invent penicillin or write *Pot-Bouille* instead. But little Josée? We'd never know. Life's shit.

As for the others, there was a man and a woman, both in their forties; I'd never seen them before. And a young woman, impossible to recognize: her head was crushed. I said what had to be said, signed what had to be signed, and left with Angéla. I was bummed out. It was the old lady and the little girl. Especially the little girl. I took it personally. I'd done everything to hasten my own death, short of jumping off a roof or shooting myself in the head. But here I was still alive. And they were dead.

I drove Angéla back to the Bien Bon. We didn't say much. When she got out of the car, she asked my name. Then she said:

– One day at time, Gérard. *Un jour à la fois*. Take care of yourself.

A sister in the struggle.

All of a sudden, life became too much to bear. Just like that, for no particular reason. Because there was a child's corpse in the fridge on rue Parthenais. Because I had to start all over again from scratch, one more time. Because I had rolled my rock to the top of the hill and now it was rolling back down again. All the times before, I'd managed to put on a brave face. But there comes a time when you just don't feel strong enough to look for another place to live and go shopping again for clothes and dishes and cutlery and scouring pads and toilet paper. This was one of those times. When I got back to the hotel, I asked the Barbie at reception for the key to the mini-bar. It burned in the palm of my hand. I slapped it back down on the counter and ran out. I had to find a meeting.

I pulled myself together in a church basement in Verdun, at an English meeting. French, English, Tamil, or Algonquin, it really doesn't matter: all AAs have the same story. Sometimes I tell myself that's all it means to be AA: to invent a story that makes sense of the wreckage of your life. To make up a story and tell it to a group. You pluck up the courage, you get up, you walk to the front of the room, you look at the gathering, ten, twenty, fifty losers just like you, and you say:

– Hi. My name is Gérard and I'm an alcoholic.

Then you tell your story. It's the same story the woman before you told or the guy after you. A story everyone's heard a hundred times before but it still feels good. A story with a beginning (the downfall), a middle (hell), and no end. Because when you're an alcoholic you walk a tightrope and even if you stay sober for ten years you'll never know how the story's going to end. So you keep digging hard in the corners, you keep practicing the Twelve Steps, and you know it'll never be easy. One day at a time, every day. 24/7, 365.

Stories are sacred.

I'm unsure about a lot of things in life, but I know stories are sacred. *L'Assommoir, Germinal,* the Bible, or an AA story, they all serve the same purpose: they impose order on chaos. Telling a story is like whistling in the dark when you're afraid. It's making music in the void. We tell stories so we don't kill ourselves. Three hundred thousand people a day used to read my stories in the *Journal de Montreal* and I'm ashamed to say that not once in 30 years did I give them a true story. All my stories about rapes, murders, kidnappings, accidents, and disasters left my readers with nothing but fear, emptiness, and a sense of powerlessness. Placed end to end, my collected works would have made a good advertising campaign for suicide.

That night in Verdun I didn't speak. I listened to my suffering brothers and sisters. I admired their strengths and feared for their weaknesses. And I went back to the hotel sober. One day at a time. I went straight to bed but after six cups of coffee I couldn't sleep. I kept saying over and over to myself: stories are sacred, stories are sacred. I think it was that night I got the idea: to write a story about the explosion on rue Darling, just for me. To try to make sense of the absurdity of it. To bring back to life those six people who'd died for nothing, like I bring back to life my own dead for a while, my mother and father, when I think about their life of poverty and try to convince myself it was a good life (even if it's not true). Stories are the only eternity an agnostic like me can believe in.

For once in my life, I was going to make a good story out of the news. So I wouldn't drink. So I wouldn't kill myself.

◆

The next morning I got up excited for the first time in a long time. It's amazing how having a purpose greater than yourself can change your outlook. For seven months I'd been completely focussed on my problems, on staying away from the bottle and moving forward in my understanding and practice of the Twelve Steps. That and just taking care of myself, eating better, keeping myself and my apartment clean. I'd also read *Les Rougon-Macquart* twice from beginning to end. I'd been going in circles. All of a sudden, it was as if all my old reflexes kicked back into gear. I phoned my old contacts at the fire department and the coroner's office. Then I made an outline of what I knew:

Six dead.

Four identified: Adrienne Dumas, the old lady on the first floor (identified by a friend); little Josée and her mother Denise (identified by Denise's mother, a Madame Laperrière, who lived in the neighbourhood); and the mother of the student, a woman by the name of Diane Demers.

Two unidentified: a man in his forties, found near Madame Demers; and the mystery woman with the squashed head. No one was even close to identifying her.

Besides the dead, there was one tenant missing: my neighbour on the third floor, a sales clerk in a store. There was no trace of him.

And there was no news, either, of the guy with the beard. His name was François Gravel. He'd checked out of the hotel where they'd taken us after the fire and left no forwarding address.

I went to the Bien Bon for breakfast. I told Angéla what I had learned but she didn't seem very interested. I told her I was starting to get a hunch about the student's lie and why she had run away from us at the morgue. Then she cut me off:

– It's none of your business, Gérard. Let the dead lie in peace. You've got no right digging around in other people's lives. Besides, what good is it going to do you? You'll only hurt yourself. And you're going to hurt other people, too.

It was the longest speech I'd heard from her in seven months and it knocked the wind out of my sails. All my high-minded reveries about stories and truth didn't seem so high-minded anymore.

– I just want to know, that's all. They were my neighbours.

– I bet you never even talked to them.

She turned her back on me and started stacking dishes. She was deliberately ignoring me. Fine. End of conversation. I opened the *Journal* and scanned the obituaries. Madame Adrienne Dumas, age 88, widow of the late Paul-Émile Potvin, survived by her nephews and nieces. Visitation at the Sansregret funeral home on rue Ontario. It was almost next door, I'd drop in later. There was also a photo, *très chic*, of a woman in a short black dress with a pearl necklace: Madame Diane (Pilon) Demers, MD, age 46, from accidental causes. Wife of Monsieur Claude Demers. Sadly missed by her daughter Hélène, her sisters Paule and Juliette, and several brothers-in-laws, nephews, and nieces. No visitation. Funeral service to be held at Saint-Viateur d'Outremont church on Wednesday, October the 12th, at 10:00 o'clock. Wow! The major leagues! The Demers of the National Bank and the Quebec Liberal Party. Now why would this guy's wife have died in a shabby apartment in Hochelaga?

At that moment Lieutenant Geoffrion walked in, head down, looking like a beaten dog. He ordered a toasted cinnamon bun with butter. He didn't notice me sitting there. Obviously I wasn't making much of an impression on anyone that morning.

– What's up? I said.

He swung around on his stool.

– What are you doing here?

– It's my *chez moi*. I took up residence here after my place blew up.

– Oh yeah, right. You lived on Darling.

He stuck his nose back in his cup and waited for his cinnamon bun. Not much for small talk, our Boomer.

– How's the investigation going, lieutenant?

– Nada.

– What do you mean, nada?

– Nada. Nothing. *Rien.* Ziltch. I've never seen one like it. *Absolument rien.* It's like a gas explosion, except there was no gas. The building wasn't even hooked up to the main.

– An underground leak?

– You want my job?

– *Non, non.*

His bun arrived. I let him eat in peace. Then I asked him:

– How much longer are you going to stay on the case?

– As long as it takes.

Lieutenant Geoffrion got up and pulled on his coat, then muttered under his breath:

– What I don't get is the streaker.

– The what?

– The streaker. Just before the place blew up, the woman across the street saw a guy running on the roof, stark naked.

The Boomer walked out.

He didn't have to tell me which woman across the street. She was in her fifties, a beanpole with flaming orange hair. She spent her whole life on the balcony (in summer) or at her window (in winter), just watching people. A human surveillance camera. I left the Bien Bon, walked over to Darling, and climbed the stairs to her place.

– *Bonjour* Monsieur Langlois, she said with a big smile as she opened the door.

I was astounded.

– How do you know my name?

One simple question and she was off and running.

– I've known your name for years! When you moved in across the street I couldn't believe my eyes. I read your stories every day in the *Journal de Montreal.* Your photo was always above your column. You really had a way with words when it came to murders. That young guy who replaced you isn't half as good. That explosion was awful, eh? If you ask me, it was something to do with drugs. The Hells Angels were after the guy with the beard, I'm positive! Have you found another place to live? I have a room to rent if you're looking. Just say the word. Come in, come in, *entrez!* What can I do for you? Welcome to my little museum!

She took me into the living room. It was overflowing with elephants: porcelain ones, cuddly ones, bronze ones, plastic ones; big ones, little ones, and a few gigantic ones. There was one made out of shells (a souvenir from Atlantic City), one made out of popsicle sticks, and one painted on velvet. There were ashtray elephants, candy dish elephants, and one that could have been a telephone. Maybe it trumpeted instead of ringing.

– I collect them. People give them to me. My big dream is to own a real carved tusk, but that's a no-no, eh?

Seen up close, she didn't look in her fifties anymore. I gave her at least seventy. She was wearing houndstooth tights, a fuchsia mohair sweater, and cats-eye glasses that sparkled. She chain-smoked Export A's (unfiltered) and coughed like she was going for a Guinness world record. On the table beside the window were a pair of opera glasses. The telescope was probably stashed under the sofa. A real nut case.

– Sorry, I didn't catch your name.

– Madame Kovacs. Marie-Rose Kovacs. My family name was Durocher. Monsieur Kovacs died in 1958. We were married young.

I had a flash of Monsieur Kovacs escaping back to Hungary, preferring life under Communism to living with Marie-Rose.

As it turned out, she had seen – "by accident, you understand" – a naked man running across the roof a few seconds before the explosion.

– It's pretty strange, eh? I mean, in the middle of October.

As if it's more common to see streakers on the rooftops in the middle of summer.

– Completely naked? You sure? Not a stitch on him?

– *Ah oui*, I could swear to it.

With her opera glasses, no doubt.

– You didn't happen to recognize him?

– It was dark, you know. And besides, he was running fast.

– So he got blown up, too?

– *Non, non.* He made it to the next building in time.

– What was that you were saying about the Hells Angels?

She'd been dying for me to get to that.

– The big guy, you know, your downstairs neighbour, the guy with the beard, he sold drugs. *Un dealer.* I'm sure of it. He went out three or four times a night and always drove off in his big red sports car with no muffler. He wasn't going to deliver pizzas, *garanti!*

– You actually saw that?

– Every night. Without fail. And look, come on, he didn't buy a new sports car every year with his welfare cheque.

I didn't ask if she got any sleep at night.

Madame Kovacs was certain the Hells Angels had bombed the house to bump off the guy with the beard, in her estimation a moron who beat his wife ("a nice, friendly woman – I don't know what she was doing with a guy like that") and shouted at his kids ("it's the drugs, eh? – it makes them crazy").

–– Hang on a minute, Madame Kovacs. If what you're saying is true, you'd have seen something suspicious, wouldn't you?

She was offended.

– Do you think I spend my whole life loitering at the window?!

OK, bad choice of words. I toned it down a bit and tried again. I asked if she had noticed anything unusual in the building across the street.

– Apart from the guy with the beard, no. I mean, you, you're always reading your Bible. And you don't eat at home much. The guy beside you on the third floor seems to be really quiet, but his curtains are pretty thick. The young woman on the second floor, the student, she seems to be pretty quiet, too, but... ah ...

– Ah ...?

– Well ... when she's not there, sometimes a woman goes in. And a man joins her. *Une femme riche,* with a big car. The man arrives in a taxi. When they're finished, they leave separately.

– And you're pretty certain that ...

– Come on, I wasn't born yesterday! But I didn't see anything, you understand. They drew the curtains.

– Of course. And the old woman on the first floor?

– Madame Dumas? A saint, *une sainte femme!*
What a shame ...

◆

Lieutenant Geoffrion was sitting in his Fire Department
van when I left Madame Kovac's. He had a smirk on
his face.

– A fruitcake, eh?

– A fruitcake, lieutenant. Did she tell you her
theory about the Hells Angels?

– *Oui.*

– What do you think?

– It was no bomb. I'll bet my life on it.

Betting his life: the Boomer didn't use words like
that lightly. Before he got promoted to investigator,
he was a firefighter, a rank-and-file, bottom-of-the-
heap grunt. One Christmas Eve he got trapped by
a fast-moving blaze and had to jump out a third-
floor window in flames. There's more titanium in
his legs than bone. They used skin from his ass to
patch up his hands. He's made of strong stuff, our
Boomer. And he believes in miracles.

– Still no idea what caused it?

– Still no idea. *Salut.*

Lieutenant Geoffrion isn't happy not knowing the

cause of a fire. It puts him in a bad mood. He rolled up his window and drove away.

I went back to the Bien Bon and started going through the classifieds. I only had one more free night at the hotel and it was time to find a new place to live. Angéla was watching me out of the corner of her eye.

– Are you still looking for a place around here? There's a two-and-a-half for rent above my place. It looks pretty clean. An old lady used to live there.

– Where's your place?

– 3465 Lafontaine.

If someone had told me that a street address could trigger an adrenalin rush, I'd never have believed them. But that's what happened. 3465. I could picture exactly where it was: right across the street from my childhood home, my old yard, and the old plum tree. 3465 was an apartment building, built in the fifties after a fire levelled a row of old houses. We'd spent the night on our balcony watching the firemen at work. Maybe that's when the seed of my illustrious future career was planted. 3465. When they finished the new building my mother went over to look at the apartments, out of curiosity. When she came back, she said:

– They're clean.

For her, that was the ultimate compliment. For me, it didn't matter: clean or not, I was going to rent that apartment.

The janitor was a thin, sickly man with a runny nose and glassy eyes. He took his time looking me over from head to toe. When he decided I wasn't the type to open a shooting gallery in his building, he showed me the apartment. It was perfect: from the window in the all-in-one-living room-dining room-kitchen I could see my old family home. The rent was high, but doable: three-twenty-five a month heated, fridge and stove included. That meant two less things I'd have to buy. I wrote a cheque on the spot and the janitor left me alone. I went over to the window and looked out.

The Inuit say if you get lost in a blizzard, you walk in circles and eventually you end up right back where you started.

◆

I stood at the window a long time, thinking about my dead. But I had to go on living. I'd been wearing the same clothes for two days and it was time to do something about it. I went to the Glaneuses. I like that place. There are as many stories on the racks of a second-hand clothing store as there are on the shelves in a library. The thing is, you have to want to read them, and most of the people you find at Value Village, the Salvation Army store, or the Glaneuses have too many problems with their own stories to care much about anyone else's. But I can never look at the rows of dresses, jackets, shoes, and raincoats without wondering about the lives of the people who'd worn them. Modest lives, for the most part, kind souls who would have made sure their clothes were clean before passing them on to someone harder up than themselves. Sometimes you find surprises: this blue silk dress, for example, very glamourous and low-cut, straight out of the forties. What belle of the ball had worn it? She'd be old now, or dead: perhaps her walker was one of those jumbled in the corner. And then the piles of hats: ones like your uncle used to wear, with the little feather on the side, or tweed caps with little ear flaps that tuck up inside. And the black shoes, rows of them, polished for decades by men who wore them only on Sundays. Going to the Glaneuses is like visiting an archaeological excavation of the neighbourhood, peering into a past that will never return.

I bought a yellow cardboard suitcase, some shirts and sweaters, and a few pairs of pants. While I was at it, I bought a mattress, a table and two chairs, some dishes and kitchen stuff, a reading lamp, and an old vinyl La-Z-Boy that smelled of Brylcreem, all to be delivered the next day to my new address. A volunteer asked, joking, if I'd had a fire. When I told her I'd lived at the place on Darling that blew up, she arranged it so I didn't have to pay for a thing. Her name was Gaétane Laplante. *Merci* Gaétane.

I dropped by the Bien Bon to tell Angéla we were going to be neighbbours. She seemed pleased. After a quick coffee I went over to the Sansregret funeral home. I'm not kidding, that's its real name: the Sansregret – no regrets. You couldn't have made it up. It was like Doctor Payne from my childhood days. ("Adélard, the kid's running a temperature of a hundred and four! Quick, call Doctor Payne!"). In these days of multinational funeral companies listed on the stock exchange; pre-paid, air conditioned columbaria; and funeral homes with multiculti chapels, day-care centres, and lounges fitted with video games, it does the heart good to know there's still a family-run business that has respect for both the dead and the wallets of the living. At the Sansregret, there's nothing chichi. They dispatch your dearly departed with dignity and economy. Death is serious stuff, but everyone knows you've still got to pay the rent on the first of the month.

I was surprised to find an open casket. There she was, Adrienne Dumas, the saint, a tiny, beautiful old woman asleep on a satin bed, a crystal rosary entwined in her folded hands. She looked at peace. That's not usually the case with disaster victims; their faces are usually etched with pain. I don't know why, but I was moved. I knelt down in front of the casket and pretended to pray. Maybe it counts, for something.

After a moment, I heard a familiar voice behind me:

– Did you know her?

I turned around. It was a woman in her forties. I couldn't place her.

– *Pas beaucoup, non*. We were neighbours. I was away when the building blew up.

– Lucky you.

– *Oui, je suppose*. Was she your mother?

– My aunt.

– I wished I'd got to know her better. Would you mind telling me a little about her?

She didn't have to be asked twice. She adored her aunt Adrienne. After a minute, it clicked, that beautiful voice: it was the weather lady on the FM. I guess even those kinds of people have dear little old aunts, too.

Adrienne was from the neighbourhood. She'd been born on a farm but her family had moved to the city during the Depression. Adrienne only got as far as fourth grade, then she went to work at the Viau Biscuits factory. She married late, at 37. Her husband was a mailman. They'd met 20 years earlier at a Young Catholic Workers meeting but had lost touch. The mailman was very religious, an austere man, a churchwarden in the parish, and a knight of the Order of the Holy Sacrament. He coached youth sports. They didn't have children of their own. Adrienne was always cheerful; it was her nature. She submitted to her husband's sternness, but never became bitter.

– She was a *sainte femme*, as we say, but she never moralized. At 37 she accepted the husband she could get and she made her peace with it. She loved him. He had some good qualities, my uncle Paul, even if he was a little sanctimonious. He died young and Adrienne never considered remarrying. She was a good person, I don't know how else to put it. For a long time she visited seniors in their homes. She adopted four or five or them. She did their shopping and washed their dishes, even though she was older than they were. And then her eyesight started to go. She became a prisoner in her home. In the end she only had a little peripheral vision left. She would sit about six inches from the TV, to one side of it, and that way she could still follow her shows. But she kept house with almost no help from anyone. She knew where everything was. She could make her own meals without spilling things. She did her own cleaning. She was so afraid we'd put her in a senior's residence that she did everything she could to make her place look perfect ... We would never have put her in a home.

– Did she think about death much?

– She talked about it. But she was in no hurry.

She used to say, if I keep my marbles and I don't go too deaf, I'm ready to live to a hundred. What she liked most was listening to audio books. She got them from the Magnétothèque. She was probably listening to one when the explosion happened.

A life as simple and beautiful as a tree. I don't know why, but it got to me. I choked up for a minute, which is definitely not my style. I thanked Miss Weather Lady, offered my condolences, and left. In the hallway I passed a little old lady dressed in garish colours. She often comes into the Bien Bon in the morning to have the poor man's pudding. I said hello and went out. I didn't have anything else to do, so I wandered around the neighbourhood for a while. Then I got the idea to phone the Magnétothèque and find out what Adrienne had been listening to the night she died. The young woman who answered seemed surprised by my question and I had to explain the circumstances, but then she found Adrienne's file and told me:

– It was *Trente Arpents* by Ringuet.

I'd read it in school. I went to the Maison de la culture, borrowed the book, and took it back to my hotel room.

I was awake the whole night. I couldn't put it down. The sad story of Euchariste Moisan, a poor *habitant* farmer who raises his family through sheer determination on a strip of land beside the St. Lawrence

River – it reminded me of Adrienne's childhood. And when I got to the part where Euchariste is an old man living with one of his sons in exile in the United States, surrounded by grandchildren who can't speak a word of French, it reminded me of *Un Canadien errant*, my father's favourite song. By the time I finished the book I realized that, compared with Euchariste and Adrienne, I'd had it easy. It was time to stop whining about my life.

It was light before I fell asleep. I kept thinking about Adrienne's last night. I wondered whether she'd said grace before her last supper, and how she'd served herself soup without spilling it. I wondered whether she'd done the dishes right away or left them till morning. I pictured her moving carefully to the living room, settling into her favourite arm-chair, and turning on the tape recorder. *'Charis usually made no reply to this teasing, which was the only form of tenderness they knew. All the delightful caresses, which married people are allowed, were kept for the evening, when Mélie had gone to sleep upstairs and they had closed the door of their room. Then Euchariste would suddenly take Alphonsine round the waist with a bold clumsiness which she would resist with an eager laugh. But in the daytime they dared not kiss each other because of a kind of bashfulness which made them look away when the impulse came to them. Sometimes, though, desire would come upon them in the dimly lit workshop, where Euchariste was repairing a piece of harness, or in the loft, amid the heavy odour of hay, and she would come out, fixing her hair, to be met by a smile and a sidelong glance from Mélie.* Maybe she fell asleep listening to it. And then there was a big noise and maybe a flash of light, then a moment of pain and it was all over.

◆

I must have looked pale when I walked into the Bien Bon the next morning. Angéla tried to be discreet, but I could feel her watching me with a knowing eye. I felt obliged to say something:

– Don't worry, Angéla. I read late, that's all.

I didn't know whether to feel pleased or annoyed by her concern. To avoid having to think about it, I started telling her about Adrienne. Suddenly, a hoarse voice interrupted me from the door:

– I knew Adrienne well! *Bonjour monsieur,* I saw you at the funeral home yesterday.

– *Bonjour.*

– *Bonjour,* Madame Poupart, said Angéla.

It was the little old lady I'd passed in the hall. She came in wearing a bright red coat, a yellow dress with ruffles, and a pair of children's blue rubber boots with baby ducks on them. She couldn't have been more than four feet tall. Perched on her head was a kind of bonnet that looked like one of those toilet roll covers women crochet out of Phentex. Her glasses were as thick as Coke bottles and her voice was beyond description: a kind of cavernous croaking interspersed with little girls' giggles.

– Gee, we had lots of fun together, *elle pis moi*. We travelled all over Quebec!

– Oh ya?

Two simple words. That's all it takes to open the floodgates when someone's dying to tell you their story. A simple "Oh ya?" and – *paf*! – you get ten years of a life, free of charge.

I quickly discovered there was a hole in Miss Weather Lady's account, a big fat hole of about ten years between the Viau cookie factory and marriage to the knight of the Order of the Holy Sacrament. One day, it seems, Adrienne got fed up packing Whippets in boxes and signed on with a burlesque company. The guy who ran the company, a Monsieur Gignac, recruited her at an amateur contest. Madame Poupart's face lit up as she told the story. She was remembering the best years of her life.

– We were chorus girls! We sang, too. Her stage name was Hattie. We played every village in Quebec and every *petit-Canada* in the States. We did shows in parish halls and split the money 50-50 with the priests.

The girls were poorly paid, poorly housed, and kept on a tight leash by the boss's wife who was in charge of the troupe's morals. After three years on the road, Adrienne disappeared, so to speak. A few years later, Madame Poupart bumped into her by accident in Montreal and they started spending time together again. Little by little, the truth emerged: Adrienne had become the mistress of a prominent, married man. He'd kept her, in modest style.

– He was the love of her life. She never told me his name. Things were different then, it wasn't like today. Anyway, he died, I don't know what of, and Adrienne went back to the cookie factory. She lived on her own for a long time, and then she met Paul. She told him everything about her past. He married her anyway. He never reproached her for anything. But he didn't like her spending time with her old friends, so we didn't see each other again for thirty years, until *he* died. That really broke her up. She really loved him. *Moi, personellement,* I didn't exactly find him the life of the party. But then I wasn't in the bedroom with them.

With that, she gave us a big crocodile wink, popped the last bit of pudding in her mouth, and got up to leave.

– Adrienne was one of a kind. Gee, we had fun together, she was a barrel of laughs. Well, bye-bye kiddies!

She was out the door in a flash, as light on her feet as a schoolgirl. I looked at Angéla.

– Beautiful story, eh?

– *Oui.* But don't count on the others being the same.

She walked away, leaving me to my coffee. The phone rang. It was for me. It was my contact at the coroner's office. He told me that a woman named Caron had claimed the body of the mystery man, and that little Josée and her mother Denise had been identified the day before by Denise's mother. I asked for their contact details and decided to go see Denise's mother right away. She lived in the neighbourhood. I was just heading out the door when Angéla, looking angry, called after me:

– You and I'd better have a talk one of these days!

I smelled it as soon as I stepped into the stairwell: the sure sign of a binge. A rancid odour of beer, sweat, sugar, and vomit. It hit me like a fist in the gut. A rush of visceral memories swept over me: years of mornings-after-the-night-before, waking up in hospital or in a grotty tourist room, shirt filthy, underwear stained, hair matted. Proust had his *madeleines,* for me it was the smell of a binge. Anyone who thinks alcohol is glamourous has never seen the bottom of a third forty-ouncer of Scotch.

The lady of the house was out of it. She mistook me for the delivery boy from the *dépanneur* on the corner.

– You got my bottles of Rossini?

Yech. The only good thing about Canadian vermouth is that it's 18 per cent alcohol and you can have it delivered from the *dépanneur*. It's the end of the line for alcoholics. Next stop, delirium tremens. I set Madame Laperrière straight about who I wasn't and climbed the stairs. She was waiting for me at the top, swaying on her feet, barely focussing. I helped her back inside. Big mistake. I should have known that the only thing you get from someone that drunk is trouble.

The apartment looked like a war zone. Ashtrays knocked over, broken chairs and glasses, blood stains on the carpet and walls, a half-burnt cushion in a corner, dirty clothes all over the place. The decor of a rock-bottom alcoholic. The lady of the house was wearing an Ottawa Senators T-shirt, boxer shorts with little hearts on them, and slippers with pink pom-poms. She was probably forty but looked seventy-five. I don't know why, but the commercials by Educ'alcool are never that realistic. I sat Madame Laperrière down on the sofa. She closed her eyes for a moment; her head must have been spinning. Then she looked at me.

– Who are you?

– A neighbour of your daughter Denise. I came to offer my condolences.

– Well, shove them up your ass! She got what she deserved. Tough titty!

It was her own daughter she was talking about. Anyone with a brain in their head would have walked out at that point. I stayed.

– Why do you say that, Madame Laperrière?

– She became a real smart-ass when she started going to university. Started shitting all over us. We weren't good enough for her. She moved to the west end and got an unlisted number.

Madame Laperrière burst into tears. Then she stopped.

– For fuck sake, isn't there anything to drink around here?

I brought her a glass of water. She drank it absent-mindedly then put the glass down in mid-air, six inches from the edge of the table. Fortunately, it was almost empty. I tried to steer her back to Denise.

– Your daughter. Why did she move back to the neighbourhood?

She looked at me suspiciously.

– Who are you?

– I told you, a neighbour.

– So how come you're not dead?

– I don't know ... Why'd Denise come back to the neighbourhood? Was it a guy?

– That fucking François can go fuck himself!

– Why do you say that?

Not a word. She clammed right up. I tried another approach.

– Tell me about your grand-daughter. What's her name?

Bad move. Madame Laperrière muttere   d'
and broke down completely. She hunched   w
began rocking back and forth, sobbing out of
Then, just as suddenly, she leapt to her feet and
throwing everything she could get her hands o

   – Madame Laperrière, *calmez-vous*. Mayb
should lie down, sleep a little.

   I tried to settle her on the sofa. Before I knew
had her arms around me and was pulling me down o
of her. It was revolting. I'd just managed to disenta
myself and calm her down a little when a huge n
appeared, steadying himself against the wall. He w
in his sixties, a beached whale in his one-piece Penm
long johns. He glared at me with glazed eyes.

   – What the fuck's going on?

   I didn't stick around for the introductions. I wa
out the door in a flash.

   *Having had a spiritual awakening as the resu
of these Steps, we tried to carry this message to othe
alcoholics.* The twelfth and final step. I never got tha
far. It would have taken someone a lot stronger tha
me to help the people I'd just run away from, thoug
God knows they needed all the help they could get.
headed over to rue Lafontaine to wait for the furnitu
delivery. On the way, I passed my old place on Darlin
Lieutenant Geoffrion's van was still parked out fron
He must have been rooting around under the rubbl

isting off a piece of gyproc with a make-up brush, orking by flashlight. It takes all kinds, I guess.

A voice called out from above:

– Monsieur Langlois! Monsieur Langlois!

It was Madame Kovacs, perched on her third-floor balcony.

– He's back!

– *Qui ça?*

– The man with the beard. He came back to get his car. It was parked at the corner of Adam.

– You saw him?

– No, but his car is gone. It was either him or the other guys.

– What other guys?

– You know ...

She mouthed the words "Hells Angels."

– Ah, OK. I'll look into it. *Merci,* Madame Kovacs!

I couldn't take any more. I went back to my new home and sat on the floor in the middle of the living room-dining room-kitchen. There's something deeply comforting about an empty room. It's like being on the prairies, or on a beach: you can see trouble coming a long way off. I should've seen trouble coming in my empty room; I was alone and there was nothing to distract me. I should've started making a searching and fearless moral inventory of myself (Step Four). Instead, I was fixated on Denise and her little Josée.

It sounded like the classic story of a young woman trapped by her milieu. Denise had obviously been a good student. She'd gone to CEGEP and then on to university, probably against her mother's advice (or, more likely, in the face of her mother's complete indifference). She'd broken with her family to get on with her life. And then, who knows, maybe she'd run into problems at university, gone back to the kind of bar she'd frequented as a teenager, and fallen for the first bum who reminded her of her father or the old neighbourhood. Preferably a bum with a drug or alcohol problem so she could imagine saving him. And then she died, for no reason, in an accident with no apparent cause. An absurd tale, if ever there was one. Worse, it might have been true. But one thing I still couldn't figure out: where was her lover man, François, missing for two days then coming back for his car? Flying high, probably, cranked up on coke. Too stoned to know what was happening. Or staying stoned, so he wouldn't have to think about it.

The truck from the Glaneuses arrived with my new living environment (as they say in *Décormag).* I arranged my furniture, which didn't take long considering the elegant simplicity of my tastes. Then I had a shower and changed my clothes. I cut a fine figure of a man in my new, slightly-used shirt and my new, previously-owned pants (both striped, though unfortunately the stripes were going different ways). I was set for life. I tried out my La-Z-Boy to kill time before dinner. And I promptly fell asleep.

◆

Someone was knocking at the door. For most mortals, that's nothing unusual. For me, it was earth-shattering. No one ever visits me. Don't get me wrong, I'm not complaining. I know where to find people when I want them. I climbed out of my La-Z-Boy ready to send packing the Jehovah's Witnesses, or the Boy Scout selling chocolate bars, or the ex-con rehabilitating himself by peddling ballpoint pens, or anyone else who thought they had the right to disturb my peace of mind and home. I flung open the door. Angéla barely managed to pull the dish she was holding out of the way.

– Am I disturbing you?

– I was sleeping.

– *Excusez-moi*. I brought you a potato pie. I figured you wouldn't be set up for cooking yet.

She came in, a fine-looking woman in her forties, a little chubby perhaps, a little worn out. She had thick cascades of black hair, a slight rasp to her voice, and an accent with traces of the sea. And she was still addressing me as *vous*, since I was old enough to be her father.

Angéla cast an eye over my living environment.

– You haven't got much.

– I like it that way. We're always dragging too much stuff around with us.

She knew what I meant: she looked like she'd been dragging around enough stuff of her own. I asked her if she wanted to join me for dinner. She had to go back to her place to get the salt and napkins and other things I didn't have. Then we attacked the potato pie.

– Is this a recipe from back home?

– *Oui*. A poor man's dinner.

– When I was a kid, we used to put salmon in it.

– I guess you weren't as poor as we were.

We shovelled in potatoes for a moment.

– So, how'd you end up in Quebec, Angéla?

Silence. I wasn't going to get her story that night.

– The important stuff, you already know. The details, I'll tell you another time. What about you? You told me yesterday you were born just across the street?

So that was the deal: a potato pie for the story of my life. Normally, I would have told her to drop it, but I wasn't in a normal state of mind. I have to admit, she was having an effect on me. So I poured it all out: my three marriages, my brilliant career covering the local police beat, my half a swimming pool full of

Scotch, the whole enchilada. Two or three times she said: "I know what you mean ..." and she sounded like she did. When I got to the end of my story and we'd drained the second pot of coffee, I asked her why she was asking me so many questions.

– Because you're an interesting person. And I like stories, too. But I prefer stories about people who are still alive. It's good to take an interest in the living. More than the dead.

Oh, oh. I could sense something coming.

– Why do you say that?

– Because you worry me, snooping around, asking all your questions.

– *C'est mon affaire.*

– No argument there. But if you ask me, I think you're just playing reporter again and sticking your nose in where it's none of your business.

– I could have died that night. I have a right to know what happened!

– What difference will it make if you find out? Do you think we'll ever know why some people die and other people live? Haven't you got enough to do right now, just looking after yourself and the people around you?

She got up.

– I've got to get some sleep. I get up at five. Easy does it, *mon ami.*

End of conversation. Exit the beautiful Acadian woman, leaving behind a guy in his sixties, confused and insomniac, in an empty kitchen with dirty dishes and no dish soap.

◆

I loathe rue Laurier. It's bad enough on the Plateau, where two thirds of the residents dress in black and three quarters of them are novelists, scriptwriters, painters, dancers, multimedia artists (whatever the hell that means) or tightrope show-offs from the Cirque du Soleil. On Laurier between Christophe-Colomb and Papineau you get the impression that half the population of Quebec is rehearsing a show for the other half. Thank God for grants. OK, sure, the guy at the artisan bakery makes bread, and I might actually get to like him if he'd stop trying to sell me his philosophy along with his *baguettes*. But at least he's making something. Which is more than you can say for the ladies of Outremont, wiggling their anorexic little asses on Laurier west of Saint-Laurent. It's even worse in that quarter-mile stretch of Laurier in Outremont. Everything I hate most in the world is right there, in full view. Ah, the delectable pleasures of class hatred! I start hating them when they double-park their cars (four possibilities: BMW,

Mercedes, Volvo, or a 4-by-4 as big as a cruise ship).
I hate them more when they turn on their car alarms
that honk as they walk away. I hate them when they
stop and yack on their cell phones in the middle of
the sidewalk, like they own the place. I hate their
áccent (floating around in mid-Atlantic, somewhere
between Paris and Montreal). I hate them when
they give to panhandlers and I hate them when they
don't. I hate their Benetton kids, with enough money
in their mouths in orthodontics to feed a village in
Burkina Faso for a decade. I hate the men in their
three-piece suits and the women in their chic little
business outfits. I hate their Saturday pullovers and
loafers even more. I hate the way they talk like they
own the world. I hate the way they size you up in
a glance (what's *he* doing here?). I hate the brown-
nosers and cocksuckers who work in their chrome
boutiques and try to sound like they're from Paris; I
hate even more the ones who don't have to try. I hate
their vulgar power and their boorish confidence. I
wish them nothing but the worst and I long for the
good old days of that great Chinese invention: re-
education through manual labour.

One Christmas Eve, back in the days when bombs
were going off in mail boxes around town, Chantal and
I went to midnight mass at Saint-Viateur d'Outremont
church, at the end of rue Laurier. It's a real in-your-

face church, glittering with gold from dome to altar, the perfect catwalk to model your new mink coat. The principal object of devotion there is social rank and I'll bet you no one has ever confessed to exploiting his workers, screwing the maid, selling his soul, or double-crossing a business partner. That night half the political elite of Canada and Quebec was strutting around the nave in their raccoon skin coats. It seems I was more than a little intoxicated and talking in more than a whisper when I proclaimed that the FLQ should have planted one of their bombs there. To avoid a scandal, Chantal steered me towards the door. Bad move. Imagine my delight when I came nose-to-nose with Pierre Elliott Trudeau who was just then making his grand entrance. It was over in a second. I'm sorry to say I didn't get the satisfaction of planting my fist in his face, but it wasn't for lack of trying. One of his gorillas stepped between us and took my sucker-punch on his starched white shirt. Then he escorted me to a snow-bank outside so I could freshen up while he whispered something into his walkie-talkie. In English.

I was musing on that fond memory while I parked my heap on Laurier. I couldn't get it into reverse (it happens sometimes), so I got out and pushed it into a parking spot. Then I strolled over to the funeral service for the late Madame Diane Demers, trophy wife of the head honcho of the National Bank. The church hadn't changed. The service was simple, dignified, and in good taste. Everybody who was anybody was there, and not a peasant in sight – except for me, of course, looking like a pimple on a powdered ass in my nylon Canadiens windbreaker and my striped pants with the stripes going the wrong way. When the ceremony was over, the *cortège* followed the casket down the aisle. My former neighbour Hélène Demers walked beside her father, with all the dignity befitting such an occasion. She didn't look like a slumming student anymore. She carried herself with the tailored elegance of her class. She had this regal way of holding her head; this was not a woman born for ordinary things. What ensued was a minor masterpiece of non-verbal communication. Our eyes met, she looked at her father, and indicated my presence with an almost imperceptible tilt of her head. Monsieur Demers, in turn, discretely indicated my presence to a Tarzan in a three-piece suit. I wasn't kept waiting. Money is a beautiful thing, isn't it? Some loser can shout himself hoarse at the welfare office for hours without getting anywhere, but all it takes is a nod from some VIP to set in motion a two-hundred-and-fifty-pound flunkey in an Italian suit.

This time, there was no scene. The goon was waiting for me outside the door and led me aside. He spoke courteously with a trace of a Slavic accent (where do they find these guys?) and made me an offer I couldn't refuse.

– Monsieur Demers has asked me to convey to you his polite request not to disturb the family and not to publish anything about the death of Madame Demers.

He was almost charming, like a *maître d'* quietly advising a regular against the Dover sole.

– And, there is this ... to compensate you for your inconvenience.

The envelope contained ten, crisp one-hundred dollar bills. They'd done their homework: losers like me come cheap. In detective novels, this is the point at which the fallen hero atones for his sins, recovers his lost dignity, throws the money on the ground, and gets pounded to a pulp. Not me. I said OK, put the money in my pocket, and walked away.

The fact is, my Pinto needed a transmission job. And I didn't really give a shit about their story anyway. It wasn't hard to imagine what had happened: a high-rolling bourgeois woman cheats on her husband using her daughter's apartment because she thinks hotels are too risky and motels too sordid. Then she dies when the building blows up, just as she's taking off her panties. What more did I need to know? The colour of her lingerie? Whether lover boy cried "mommy" when he came? Those kind of people bore me. I drove back to Hochelaga and headed for the Caisse Populaire to deposit the cash.

You've got to allow lots of time when you go to the bank on the first of the month. It's Cheque Day. In the morning, the line snakes all the way out the door and spirits are high on the sidewalk outside. They're all there: Frail seniors who look like they've spent a month hiding in their rooms. Sixteen-year-old girls proudly pushing baby carriages. Young punks in debt to their dealers. Unemployed guys desperate to get the cable switched back on. Mothers in a hurry to fill their fridges and cook a decent meal before the kids get home from school. Immigrants right off the boat from Mars: for them, Cheque Day is like Christmas. And of course the regulars from the tavern, planning the mother of all binges. My brothers and sisters. *Mes semblables, mes frères.* My fellow citizens from the wastelands of the empire, the margins of neo-liberalism, and the ruins of the welfare state.

I decided to avoid the Bien Bon: I didn't need another lecture from Angéla. I headed for the Chez Clo instead. On the way there I ran into a group of teenagers wearing baseball caps. They were talking loud. *Ah ouan!* seemed to be their mantra.

– *Ah ouan! Ah ouan!*

– Fuck that shit was good, man!

– *Ah ouan!*

– I was out of my tree, man! Out of my fucking tree! Expressions come and go, and that one was new to me, but it wasn't hard to guess the meaning. I recognized the kid doing the bragging: it was the son of the guy with the beard. I'd seen him on the bus the night of the disaster. He couldn't have been more than twelve years old, but he already knew what he wanted to do in life: spend as much time as possible in a catatonic stupor.

– Hey! I called.

– Wha?

He was wasted. You could see it in his eyes.

– You lived on Darling, right?

– *Ouan.*

– You don't recognize me? I lived above you.

– *Ah ouan ... ouan ...*

– What's your name again?

– Patrick.

– I'm looking for your father, Patrick.

He tensed up.

– What for?

– I wanna talk to him.

– I don't know where he is.

– Where are you staying?

– At my grand-mother's.

– Madame Laperrière?

– That crazy old bag? She's not my grand-mother; she's Denise's mother.

– Do you know where your father is?

– He fucked off. I dunno know where.

– *Écoute,* Patrick. I'm just trying to find out what happened that night, the night of the explosion. Where were you when the place blew up?

– I wasn't home.

I resisted the temptation to say *"Ah ouan!"* And, eventually, I got another piece of the puzzle from him. Little Josée had run out of the house that night while her parents were fighting. They were shouting so loud they didn't hear her go. When they finally realized what had happened, everyone took off looking for her.

– I went looking, too, said Patrick. But I got lost ...

His friends thought that was hilarious.

– I came back too late. Lucky me, eh?

– Yeah, lucky you. *Écoute.* If you see your father, tell him his upstairs neighbour wants to talk to him. My name is Gérard. He can leave a message for me at the Bien Bon. Know where that is?

– *Ouan.*

– By the way, what's happening with Denise and the kid? Is someone going to bury them?

– How the fuck would I know?

He'd had enough. He and his friends walked away, the living dead, in search of new adventures in the big wide world of psychotropic drugs.

◆

Usually the pork hock stew at the Chez Clo puts things right with the world, but that day my nose was in the gravy. I was thinking about little Josée. Only three years old, but she'd had more common sense than everyone else in that dysfunctional family put together. I imagined her doing the only thing possible under the circumstances: running, leaving, getting the hell out, putting the greatest possible distance between herself and the nightmare at home.

She must have headed down Darling in her pyjamas. It was a crisp October night. Maybe she was dragging a teddy bear with her, or a blanket. She walked towards the river for a while, under the light of the street lamps; there was no one about. She was careful at the intersections, she looked left, then right, then left again, just like she'd been taught. Then she heard someone calling her name. Maybe she hid, but not well enough. Her mother found her and took her home, while her father went to the *dépanneur* for cigarettes or beer. I only hoped Denise hadn't scolded her daughter too much, that she'd hugged her tight before tucking her into bed, that there'd been enough time for a little moment of tenderness. I hoped Denise had had time to say: "Don't worry, sweetie, we won't fight any more ... there won't be any more shouting

... sleep well, *mon petit bébé* ... mommy loves you"
– before death took them both. But maybe that was
asking too much.

And now their bodies were lying in the morgue,
unburied, unclaimed, like slaughtered animals. I
thought about the people in India who believe that,
when a body is unburied, its soul wanders the earth,
troubling the living. And then there was Patrick, a lost
puppy without a collar, alive only because he was too
stoned to find his way home, but already dead, already
dead ... And his father, that jackal with a beard, gone
God knows where in his fancy drug dealer's car, a
man who didn't even have the humanity to bury his
woman and his little girl.

God, give me the strength to get through the day,
I thought. God, take away my thirst. I had to walk, to
keep moving. I left the Chez Clo and headed for the
mountain. I just put one foot in front of the other.
Maybe Angéla was right, and I should have let the
dead lie. The stories I had so far were mostly my
imagining. I'd probably never be able to prove that
Madame Demers had met a lover at her daughter's
place, or that Patrick's father was a drug dealer. And
even if I could, so what? What difference would it
make? Knowing the truth wouldn't bring me peace
of mind. I told myself I'd be better off forgetting my
pointless search and working on my Twelve Steps

instead, trying to find some measure of serenity. You don't get there by inspiration, it takes perspiration. It's hard work, day after day, 24/7, 365. It was the first day of the rest of my life, I told myself. One day at a time.

Sometimes, the clichés they spout at AA really piss me off, even if I know they're the only thing keeping me sober and alive. Sometimes I step back and look at AA with a double shot of irony. I start feeling superior to all that kitchen-table philosophy with its Hallmark sayings. And then I remember that that's why I almost ended up dead. I can spin circles in my head faster than a moth flapping around a 100-watt bulb. I mistake cynicism for intelligence. I have to remind myself that it's better to be naive and sober than brilliant and dead. I was replaying all this in my head for the thousandth time while walking up the mountain. And then all of a sudden, it hit me: it was Indian summer, the weather was gorgeous, the maples were in full colour. I had a rush of well-being. Tears flooded my eyes. It was a beautiful day, I was alive, and the light was so golden it would have made even the concrete bunkers they call high schools these days look inviting. I gave thanks. I sat down on a park bench and watched the young people go by. And then I fell asleep. At my age, and with my mileage, you can't have two late nights in a row without paying for it.

The rain woke me. It was getting dark and the wind had picked up. Autumn was back. I had fallen asleep on the far side of Beaver Lake. By the time I ran to the bus stop I was shivering like a wet poodle locked out of the house in January. In the bus shelter there was a guy in his fifties who had seen better days. He was wearing a turquoise jogging outfit and he was slumped in the corner on a canvas sack. His hair was long and greasy and he was sucking on a bottle in a brown paper bag. I nodded to him; he nodded back. I couldn't stop shivering, and after a moment he offered his brown paper bag to me, with a smile full of missing teeth.

– Here. This'll warm you up.

Cutty Sark. The devil exists, and you never know where you'll run into him. I grinned and said:

– Life is good!

– Nothing's too good for the working class. Here. *Tiens* ...

I took a deep breath.

– *Non. Merci.* I'm on the wagon. I haven't had a drop in seven months. But thanks all the same. I appreciate it.

– *Tabarnak,* he said softly. That's beautiful. That's really beautiful. *C'est très très beau* ... But don't you get bored?

The million-dollar question. I don't know an alcoholic who doesn't miss it sometimes, the binges, the parties, the brawls. I don't know an alcoholic who doesn't find life more boring sober than when he drank. I smiled.

– *Oui*, sometimes.

He nodded his head.

– Me, I'm never bored.

Silence. My new friend looked at me.

– Do you smoke?

I took out my pack, but it was soaked. The cigarettes were falling apart, the matches were useless. I threw them outside.

– Never mind, he said. God sees his little sparrow fall.

He dug into his pocket and pulled out a green plastic garbage bag.

– It's new. You just gotta make a hole for your head.

He handed it to me. The bus arrived. The Cutty Sark man didn't move.

– You staying here? I asked.

– No reason to go anywhere else.

– Thanks for the raincoat.

I pointed to the paper bag.

– Save some for tomorrow.

– Don't worry about me! And don't forget: boredom is the mother of all vices.

I gave him a thumbs-up on that point, and got on the bus.

It was dark by the time I got home. I was chilled to the bone. I emptied my pockets, peeled off my wet clothes, and had a hot bath. Then I put on all the dry clothes I owned. It still wasn't enough. I must have looked a fine sight when I opened the door to Angéla.

– I got caught in the rain.

– I know, I saw you come in. You didn't come to the restaurant today, so I figured I must have pissed you off last night with my motherly advice.

I made a vague gesture. She smiled.

– I made spaghetti. If you don't want me to think we're fighting, you'd better come down and eat at my place.

Anna Magnani! Suddenly it hit me – that's who she reminded me of. Who could turn down an invitation to eat spaghetti with the great Anna Magnani?

Angéla's apartment was as clean as a whistle, everything in its place. A few books, a few posters, a TV, a brown velour sofa, and not much else. A temporary home. On one shelf there was a kind of shrine: some shells, a jar of sand, some postcards of the beach, and photos of two boys about 10 or 12 years old.

– Yours?

– *Oui*.

It was a story as old as the world. She came from a small village on the Acadian peninsula. Her father was violent, her mother depressed, and at seventeen the only way out she could see was to get married. Her husband was a younger version of her father, a local guy who drank hard and hit hard. The day he started taking it out on the kids, she grabbed them and went to her sister's place in Moncton. Angéla found a job as a waitress, got an apartment, and bravely held the fort. At night, when the children were in bed, she made herself a vodka and orange juice to relax. Then a second one, and a third. It became a nightly ritual: never before the kids went to bed, never more than three. She was a good mother, devoted to her children. She never went out. But gradually the ratio of vodka to orange juice changed. One night the bottle was empty and she went next door to a bar, just for one. She woke up at three in the morning in a motel room with a stranger beside her in bed. She hated herself for what she had done and managed to pull herself together for a while. Then something cracked inside her.

She started drinking all night. The children would find her passed out on the kitchen floor in the morning. She started going out more, and sleeping around. She lost her job, totalled the car. The neighbours started talking. One night in July while she was out, her oldest son woke up hot and tried to open the bedroom window. The latch didn't hold and the window slammed down, cutting off his fingertip. There was blood all over the place.

His brother called 911. Angéla found a note from the ambulance crew when she got home and went straight to the hospital, drunk. Social services got involved. Her children were put in foster care. After that, it was a free-fall: coke, amphetamines, anything to get high, and twenty-dollar tricks to pay for it. One night she found a fellow hooker stabbed in an alley, her guts spilling out. Angéla realized she didn't want to die, which is the basic qualification for joining AA. But Moncton was too small to start over. So she moved to Montreal where she could disappear into the crowd without fear of running into old friends and former johns. She was leading a nun's life now, doing volunteer work at a women's shelter when she wasn't working at the restaurant or going to meetings. And she was still calling me "vous."

When I got back to my place, I stood in the dark for ages, looking out at my childhood home. I tried to put Angéla out of my mind. Clearly, she was worried about me, with the sixth sense of an alcoholic who smells trouble coming. But I didn't want her AA solicitude. And I wasn't interested in being her father figure or a substitute uncle. For want of anything better to do, I started making an inventory of things that had changed across the street. The lilac bushes must have died. The chain-link fence had been replaced with a wrought-iron one. The windows were new. The old enamelled tin plaque with the street address had been replaced with brass numbers. The solid-wood door had been replaced with a steel one. There was a crack in the front wall ... This was getting boring. I lit a cigarette and started tidying up, moving things around, opening and closing cupboards. That's when I found the piece of paper with the address and phone number of a woman named Caron, the woman who'd claimed the body of the mystery man they'd found beside Madame National Bank.

Boredom is the mother of all vices. He was dead right, my friend from the bus shelter. It was four days since the explosion and two people were still missing: the guy with the beard and my neighbour on the third floor. Four days was getting to be a long time. Were they in on some job together? And what about the woman with no face: what was she doing in the building when it blew up? And then, when I thought about it, that flunkey from the National Bank: he hadn't slipped me ten brown ones for nothing.

◆

The next morning I got back to work. I started with the landlord on Darling. He told me that my neighbour's name was Karl Godin and that Karl worked at the

Radio Shack on Ontario. The references Karl had given the landlord didn't lead anywhere: one was a phone number in Val d'Or with no answer, the other number was out of service.

The manager at the Radio Shack said Karl was a good employee, honest, dependable, and reserved. But he didn't seem to have any friends. And a change had come over him lately. He'd become irritable and had started voicing his opinion about everything. He'd missed three days straight then appeared suddenly on a Friday afternoon, agitated. He'd bought three TV sets with his credit card and left. No one had seen him since.

Clearly, something had happened to Karl. During the seven months I'd lived on Darling I'd never heard a peep from him. But the week before the explosion he'd started playing music full blast and changing the CD every few minutes. I'd knocked on his door several times but he never answered. Then he started sticking little poems on his door, on yellow Post-it notes. Strange ... I asked the manager a few more questions but there wasn't much more he could tell me. Karl's employee file at human resources in Toronto was confidential. When you know how to get it, nothing is confidential, but that takes time and money. For now I decided to drop Karl. I figured he'd show up sooner or later.

The coroner's office had nothing new for me: still no ID for the woman with no face, and no one had shown up to claim Denise and little Josée. I turned to Madame Caron. I wracked my brains trying to think of a plausible way to introduce myself so I could ask her a few questions. It's not hard to inquire about a dead neighbour or colleague: that usually doesn't arouse much suspicion or anxiety. But for someone you don't know from Eve or Adam, you've got to have a way in. I took a chance and dialled the woman's number. It was in Laval.

– Madame Caron? ... I'm a colleague of Lieutenant Gaston Geoffrion at Fire Investigation Services in Montreal. Did the lieutenant contact you? ... No? ... Well, he asked me to check some details with the relatives of the victims ... May I come and see you?

She refused outright. She had nothing to say. She didn't know what her husband was doing on Darling that night and she doubted she could help me with anything. Her voice was strange, weak and high-pitched, and she slurred her words, the way you do after you've been to the dentist. But her tone was sharp and she hung up without saying goodbye. OK. Fine. You can't always bat a thousand. I went back to work.

The Darling Tavern on Sainte-Catherine is a neighbourhood institution. For three generations it's been an obligatory stop on the way to Bordeaux prison, a community college for petty crime. (For the big time, you've got to go to law school or the

81

Hautes études commerciales.) The Darling Tavern is the scorched earth of booze joints: 25 feet by 40, brown walls, terrazzo floors, neon lights, a dozen tables, 48 chairs, a pool table, a peanut-vending machine, a few bags of potato chips clipped to a metal rack, and a Molson clock on the wall. It hasn't changed since the Korean War. You want a meal? The pizza joint around the corner delivers. You don't like Molson-O'Keefe-Labatt? Go somewhere else. You want a small glass of beer? They keep a few small glasses for fags, but don't ask for a second: you should've ordered a big one first. The waiter doesn't like walking for nothing.

I ordered a 7-Up. Nothing like making a grand entrance. When the waiter returned I asked him:

– Does François Gravel come in here sometimes?

He looked at me like an entomologist studying a bug. I added:

– The big guy, with the beard and the red Camaro.

– *Non.*

– I lived on Darling, the place that blew up. He was my neighbour. I'm looking for him.

– Keep looking.

– OK.

I stood up and put a toonie on the table but before I could take a step towards the door a voice called out from the other end of the room.

– Finish your 7-Up.

He had a blond moustache and a leather vest with fringes, a Buffalo Bill of the east end. The only thing missing was the whip and the ten gallon hat. He punched in a number on his cell phone, had a brief conversation, and then he looked at me.

– Someone is coming. It won't be long. Give him another drink, Pierrot.

Just so I'd get the message the cowboy moved to a table by the door and stuck his nose in a newspaper. I stared at my glass and wondered what hornet's nest I'd just walked into. A quarter of an hour later a man walked in. Forties, denim vest, an eagle on his belt buckle, and cowboy boots. Theme of the day. But when I saw his eyes, any impulse I might have had to kid him about his outfit evaporated on the spot. This guy was dangerous.

– I've seen you somewhere before.

My picture in *Le Journal de Montreal*. I didn't say a word.

– What do you want with François Gravel?

I winged it:

– He was my downstairs neighbour, on Darling. The place that blew up. I lent him twenty bucks in the firemen's bus. I just want it back.

He looked me over. I looked like I could use twenty bucks.

– You know him well?

– *Non*. He was just a neighbour. We were in the bus, he didn't have a penny to his name, he asked me if I could help him out, and I lent him some money. That's all.

– You don't know where he is?

– If I knew I wouldn't be looking for him.

He looked at the other cowboy with an exasperated expression and made as if he was going to leave. Then he swung back, grabbed me by the collar, and hauled me out of my chair.

– If you see him, you come back and tell Pierrot. OK?

– OK.

– OK?! he shouted, shaking me.

– OK! OK!

He let go. End of conversation. He walked out. I looked at the guy with the moustache. He motioned for me to leave.

One thing for sure, this wasn't the major leagues. This was bottom-of-the-food-chain stuff, nothing to justify an assassination attempt or a bomb. The guy who had just pushed me around had probably fronted François for a coke deal, a couple of thousand max. François had probably taken advantage of the explosion to disappear. Or maybe he was just partying hard and had forgotten all about it. Either way, I wasn't any further ahead.

I went to the Bien Bon for a coffee. Lieutenant Geoffrion was there. It didn't look like he was getting very far with his inquiries, either. He was bent over the classifieds in *Le Journal de Montreal* but he wasn't reading. The Boomer was not in a good mood.

– Still here, lieutenant?

– I'll be here next spring if it goes on like this.

– Like what?

– Someone broke into the site last night. How do they expect me to conduct a proper investigation if someone disturbs the evidence?

– The fence isn't locked?

– *Ben oui*. But not good enough.

– Any idea who it was?

He didn't answer. He had an idea. Probably the same as mine.

◆

That night I dropped in to see Madame Kovacs again. She hadn't noticed anything unusual across the street. Fair enough, she can't be at her window 24 hours a day. When I left I went around the corner and down the alley so she couldn't see me, then I walked the length of the plywood fence they'd put up at the back of the site. They'd done a half-assed job: it only took one kick to knock a plywood sheet loose and I scrambled through the gap into what was left of my old home. I pushed the plywood back into place and found a spot to hide near the foundation walls. It was a cold night. I'd gone to the Glaneuses earlier to buy a winter coat, but it wasn't going to be enough. I had a small thermos of coffee, a supply of cigarettes, and a limited amount of patience.

There are times when the sheer stupidity of something stares you in the face. I was sixty. My life was a mess. I had better things to do than freeze my balls off on a pile of bricks at one o'clock in the morning playing private detective. I could have been rereading *Nana*. Or painting my apartment. Or doing volunteer work at the Chic Resto Pop. Or, better yet, thinking seriously about how to win Angéla's heart, or at least get into her pants. I was nursing that little fantasy, telling myself that twenty years difference in age is no obstacle to love, when a faint noise jolted me out of my reverie. I pricked up my ears. More little noises. A rat.

Why on earth did I get mixed up in all this? What was I hoping to find, the meaning of life? Looking for reasons to go on living in the deaths of six complete strangers was pure masochism. We die however we die, that's just the way it is, end of story. And we live as best we can. Badly, for the most part, but we get by with whatever we have, we do the best we can. We eat, we shit, we make love if we're lucky, and we fall asleep. The next morning we get up and do it all over again. Until there is no next morning. And that's that. There is no hidden meaning to discover. For all my trouble so far I still had only a few half-baked stories riddled with holes. They were depressing stories. And the rest didn't exactly promise fun and games. I was chasing sirens again, asking questions for the sake of asking questions, following a trail just to have something to do. Anything so I wouldn't come face to face with the mother of all vices. In the meantime, I was freezing, I was shivering like a leaf, as if death was closing in. Two hours had passed. A light snow had started falling. I gave myself a good talking to and got ready to leave. I was thirsty. Tomorrow, I'd go to a meeting and have a serious talk with a veteran. I was close to falling off the wagon. I could feel it.

The plywood sheet opened with a bang and a man stepped through. It was too dark to see who he was. I shrunk into my hiding spot while he clambered down into the basement through a kind of tunnel under the rubble. He switched on a flash light: it left a halo behind him in the dust. My plan was going brilliantly. If I tried to follow him, he'd hear me. If I waited for him to come out I wouldn't be able to see his face without him seeing mine. And what if it was a face I didn't recognize? I couldn't just go up to him and ask:

– *Monsieur*, would you be so kind as to tell me your name and what you are doing in the ruins of my former home?

The situation was ridiculous. But the fact is, I was curious. I moved closer to the opening. He was inside now. He'd brought tools with him. I could hear digging and scraping, I could hear rubble being pushed aside. Then silence. And then I heard him straining to move something big. There were a couple of hits of a shovel, then more straining. I heard him swear and groan with the effort. And then there was a terrible crash as the rubble collapsed on top of him. I switched on my flashlight and started down into the tunnel. You couldn't see ten steps in front of you, the dust was an impenetrable fog. I was just about to turn back and go for help when I heard a faint moan. I couldn't just leave him there. I groped my way forward to where he was trapped. The dust began to settle. I moved some pieces of rubble and saw him, pinned under a thick beam that lay across his chest. His breathing sounded like a death rattle. It was François, the guy with the beard, my downstairs neighbour.

There was no time to lose. He was in bad shape. The beam had crushed his rib cage. And it wasn't going to be easy to move: both ends were jammed under the rubble. I told him:

– Hang in there. I'll get you out.

I put my flashlight down on the end of a cinder block and started moving bricks and pieces of wood to see if I could shift the beam. No luck. There were creaking sounds above me. The whole mountain of rubble was unstable. I thought I might have a better chance of freeing him if I cleared some space under him. I started digging and managed to move him a few centimetres. That seemed to ease the pressure on his chest. He was breathing better. But there still wasn't enough room to get his head under the beam. I kept digging. I started pulling on a 2x4 and realized, too late – wrong one! Bricks and rubble crashed down on top of me. Something hit me on the head. I found myself in complete darkness. Completely conscious. And completely panicked. I was inhaling more dust than air. I forced myself to calm down by thinking about the ocean. God knows why, I don't like the ocean.

Cigarettes cause throat cancer, lung cancer, heart disease, and stroke, not to mention social ostracism and bad breath. But smokers have one advantage over non-smokers: they've usually got a light. I dug around in my pockets while saying a little prayer for E.B. Eddy and found my book of matches. I lit one. The beam had crushed François's neck. His head was twisted at an impossible angle and his eyes were wide open. He was dead.

The cave-in had also blocked the way out. I was trapped. The match burnt my fingers. There were only three left. I lit one more to try to get my bearings. No doubt about it, I'd got myself into a real mess. I groped about in my pockets for my flashlight. No luck. I lit a cigarette. I was cold. But it didn't take a genius to figure it out: I'd just have to wait for Lieutenant Geoffrion to show up in the morning. He'd rescue me. But wait – what day was it? Friday night. Fear gripped me. Did he work Saturdays? Probably not. He probably had a bungalow in Laprairie, a wife and two kids, and a Voyager minivan. On Saturday he'd be putting on the snow tires and tuning up the snow-blower, then picking up some Kentucky Fried Chicken and hitting the sofa to watch the Canadiens get creamed by the Tyrannosauruses from Normal, Illinois. It was one thing to tough it out till morning in the company of a dead body and a few dozen rats. It was a whole other thing to sit two days freezing in the dark with nothing to eat or drink. And what if the Boomer's boss decided to close the investigation and send him somewhere else? Whoa. Calm down, Gerry boy. One day at a time.

And all this for what? A wild goose chase. I'd never know for sure what François had come looking for in the rubble, even if I figured it wasn't a few old photos of his mother. There was probably a few thousand dollars worth of coke buried a few inches from my head, fronted no doubt by his buddies at the Darling Tavern. Big deal. Big discovery. I was making great progress, stuck in this hole. Obviously, it was time to do a little introspection, to practice Step Ten: *We continued to take personal inventory and when we were wrong promptly admitted it.* If I'd had a cell phone and the number of the Power greater than ourselves, whoever we understand Him to be, I'd have called Him up right then and there: "Fine. I was wrong, *OK là?* From now on I'll be super smart, super good, super sober, super nice, and a super nobody. And I'll live to be 90. *OK? ... OK?!*"

Rebellion erupted in me. I could have howled with rage. I wanted to smash something. Instead, I chain-smoked my cigarettes, seethed with bile, and railed against Step Eleven: *We sought through prayer and meditation to improve our conscious contact with God, as we understood Him, praying only for knowledge of His will for us and the power to carry that out.* I was half mad with loathing:

– Yes, Master. Anything you say, Master. Only water for me, Master ... Christ on a fucking crutch. Enough with the boot-licking, *hostie!* I'm not a fucking poodle. *Je suis un homme!* When you fuck up and you land in shit, you get the fuck up and you start walking again. What the fuck's all this powerless shit? *Our lives have become unmanageable ... only a Power greater than ourselves can restore us to sanity.* Bullshit! I'm not sick,

I'm fucking furious! I drink because life is shit, people are bastards, and the Good Lord couldn't give a flying fuck about any of us, just like we don't give a flying fuck about cockroaches.

I was out of cigarettes. I fished around in Francois' pockets and smoked his. Then I must have fallen asleep.

When I woke up, I was three-quarters frozen and still pissed off at the world. I was stiff as a corpse. I was cramped. I was out of cigarettes, out of matches, and almost out of body heat. My fingers were numb and I couldn't feel my feet anymore. I tried moving a little. I rubbed my legs, flexed my arms, and turned my head from side to side. It was then I saw the faint light. Daybreak. In a little while there was enough to see by. I started working, very slowly, terrified I'd trigger another cave-in. After half an hour, my hands bleeding and my clothes torn, I crawled out of the rubble just as Lieutenant Geoffrion was climbing in through the fence. He looked as determined as ever but a little down in the dumps. And he didn't seem surprised to see me.

– So, it was you.

–*Non, pas moi.* You'd better call for back-up. There's another body down there, my neighbour. I saw him go in, I followed him, and there was a cave-in.

The Boomer went back to his van to call and I took the opportunity to vanish. I went home, showered, changed my clothes, and wolfed down something to eat. At 10 o'clock on the dot I was at the door of the SAQ.

◆

She was gorgeous, sitting there beside me in the car. Her curves, her golden complexion. I hadn't touched her yet, I was just imagining how warm she'd feel. I drove for the sake of driving, to prolong the pleasure, because it's always better if you hold back a little. She was waiting patiently, wrapped in her brown paper bag. I drove around the city a few of times. She loves me, she loves me not ... I wanted her so much. I parked at the look-out on Mount Royal, where the junkies and lovers go, and I gazed at the city. And then I turned to her. I pulled off her brown paper bag and read the advice printed on it: "Moderation is always in good taste." I decided that didn't apply to me. And then I looked lovingly at the yellow label and the little ship. I unscrewed the cap, thrilled by the sound I'd forgotten: click click click. And then I inhaled her aroma. And then I raised her to my lips. And then – no, not right away. I waited until the desire was unbearable. And then I think I started crying.

And then I drank.

The taste of whiskey filled my mouth. The warmth slipped down my throat. The knot in my stomach dissolved. My scalp tingled. The weight I carry on my shoulders every day from morning to night evaporated, instantly. I felt happy, truly happy, for the first time in seven months.

I was home.

◆

Staying drunk, maintaining just the right degree of drunkenness, is a high-wire act. There's a degree of intoxication that's just right. For me it's a quarter of a forty-ouncer. That much is perfect. It's peace and love, no worries, *tout cool*. But it's harder to stay right there than not to drink at all: the Sirens call from the bottle. I mustered all the willpower I had and hurled it off the look-out, then jumped back in the car. Time to move. Christ, I love driving drunk. But not in the city, on the *autoroute,* a nice and easy 90 klicks an hour in the centre lane with the turkeys flying past on both sides. Life slips into slow motion, it's all good. I was almost in Sainte-Agathe when I had a brilliant idea: finish the job. I still had Madame Caron's address, I might as well find out how that story ends. I could picture it clearly: I'd go and see her and tell her what I wanted to know. She'd either speak to me or she wouldn't, but at least I'd have tried. It's amazing how alcohol clarifies things. I took the exit at Sainte-Agathe and drove straight to the SAQ. I stashed the bottle under the seat without opening it. I was proud of my willpower. Then I pointed the car back towards Laval.

At the Porte-du-Nord I got thirsty. I pulled into the parking lot at McDonald's and downed another quarter of a bottle. It was even better than the first. You have to maintain just the right degree of intoxication, I told myself. I was about to hurl the rest of the forty-ouncer in Ronald McDonald's face, painted on the window, but I decided against it. There were people around. Besides, no use wasting good Scotch on a clown, even if he is the herald of American imperialism and prophet of the end of western civilization (whatever we understood that to be). I put the bottle back under the seat and consulted my Perly's. Madame Caron, it turned out, lived in Sainte-Rose. I headed for Sainte-Rose.

The place was beside the water, a three-story building that looked like a snake made out of bricks. The stone gate must have been ultra-modern in 1960. The sign said: "Pavillon Sainte-Béatrice: Long-Term Care." There was a garden with a pond and some maple trees in colour. A nurse was pushing an old lady around in a wheelchair. I checked the address on my scrap of paper. This was it. I went in and spoke to the woman at reception.

– Is there a Madame Caron living here?

I'll never get used to being treated with contempt. Indifference I can take, hatred I can deal with, but not contempt. She looked me over from head to toe. She looked at my Canadiens jacket, my Fortrel pants, and my crumpled scrap of paper. Her nostrils quivered and her lips pursed. I resisted the temptation to say that it was people like her that drove me to drink. Really, my willpower was amazing. There was a long silence. Then she said, yes, there was a person by that name living there.

– I'd like to see her, *s'il vous plaît.*

Another silence. Then she informed me that visiting hours began at three o'clock.

Fine, change of plan. I decided to take advantage of the delay to get my blood alcohol content down to a more socially acceptable level. It almost worked. I went to a truck stop on Route 117 and had two cups of coffee. I went to the bathroom, splashed water on my face, ran a comb through my hair, and grabbed a handful of mints at the cash. On the way out I lifted a raincoat from the cloakroom. It's important to look presentable. Then I headed back to the Pavillon Sainte-Béatrice, with another shot of Cutty Sark for the road. It's always the last one. They say people who drink are lost, but it's not true: we know exactly where we are. We're like the needle on a compass, always pointing to the bottle, our one true north. Say what you like, but it's good to have a direction in life.

The nurse who took me to Madame Caron seemed
a little concerned about my appearance. We found
her in the smoking room. She was in a wheelchair,
dressed in black. She was looking out at the trees.

– You have a visitor, Madame Caron, the nurse said.

She turned her head slowly; her movements
seemed awkward, uncoordinated. She looked at me
for a long time before speaking.

– *Qu'est-ce que vous voulez?*

– My name is Gérard Langlois. I lived in the
building where your husband died.

– Was he in your apartment?

– No.

– Did you know him ?

– No.

– Do you know what he was doing there?

– N ... no.

– So what is it you want?

Her voice was strange. It was too high, somehow,
and quivering. And yet there was authority in it, along
with unmistakable suffering and bitterness.

– *Je ne sais pas.* I'm trying to understand.

– Understand what?

The nurse caught Madame Caron's eye.

– Would you like me to show the gentleman out?

– No. Leave us alone, please.

The nurse left and Madame Caron continued.

– What is it you are trying to understand, Monsieur Langlois?

– I dunno ... I should have died, too ... It's just luck that I'm still alive ... My shoelace was undone ... It only took a few seconds to tie it ... But, because of that, I had a car accident ... I wasn't drunk ... And then, because of the accident, I got home late ... So I wasn't there when the explosion happened ... It's crazy, eh? ... I mean ... a shoelace ...

She looked at me as if I were some strange insect that had landed in her soup. I was thrown off balance. I didn't know what to say. The situation was absurd. Suddenly I realized how ridiculous I looked. I wanted to get out of there as fast as I could. I apologized and started to walk away.

– Monsieur Langlois!

I turned and faced her.

– If I understand you correctly, you're alive because your shoelace came undone.

I wanted to sink through the floor.

– And you want to know why my husband is dead, *c'est ça?* Am I wrong?

– *Excusez-moi, madame.* I didn't mean to upset you. I'll go.

I wanted to be somewhere else, anywhere else. Her expression was fierce.

– No. Don't go. I'll tell you why my husband is

dead, if that's what you want to know. My husband is dead because he went to your building to make love to another woman. Do you find that crazy, too? I know who she was, but I'm not going to tell you. He made love to her because I could no longer make love to him. Do you want me to explain that, too, Monsieur Langlois, why I couldn't make love to my husband? You want details? My medical files? The why of things interests you? There is no why, Monsieur Langlois. Life is shit, that's all. There is no why. Only the how matters. How we make love. How we cope with suffering. How our bodies fail us. Is there anything else you want to know?!

She was shouting. The nurse rushed back in to calm her, and glared at me:

– You. Out!

I retreated down the corridor. Patients came to the doors of their rooms to see what was happening. Nurses stared. The last words I heard Madame Caron screaming were "multiple sclerosis!" I turned a corner, ran down the stairs and out the lobby. The next thing I knew I was in my car, fumbling under the seat. I wanted to die.

◆

How I got to Maniwaki I'll never know. All I remember is that I was desperate to put as much distance as possible between me and what had just happened. If I'd had more guts, or been more impulsive, I'd have killed myself out of shame and despair. Happily, I had my little ship to save me. I poured Scotch down my throat and slammed my foot to the floor, trashing a couple of parked cars on the way out. I emptied my account at the first bank machine I saw then got back on the *autoroute* heading north. I must have hung a left at Grand-Remous. I vaguely remember a tavern with wood panelling and deer and moose heads mounted on the walls. Apparently some hunters wearing checked shirts came in with more heads and started measuring the antlers with tape measures. But that part's fuzzy. I only know that I drank nine hundred of the National Banks' thousand dollars and ended up in jail. The rest of the story they had to tell me.

Apparently I drank for two days straight and the waiters had to help me up to my room the first night. The next day was the close of hunting season and the hotel was hosting the Maniwaki Antler Festival, a very exclusive affair. It seems I took exception to the measuring of the antlers and climbed up on a pool table shouting: "Leave the poor animals alone!" That part I don't remember at all. And I'm surprised, really, because I've got nothing against hunting. But that's what they tell me, so it must be true. And it gets better. It seems they threw me out.

It seems I came right back in, determined to torch the winning rack. It seems I doused it in Scotch and tried to set it on fire. On the list of things not to do during the Maniwaki Antler Festival, that probably comes in at number three, right after: "Don't proposition the hunters' girlfriends" and "Don't piss off the Indians on the reserve." But a long and troubled life has taught me that tact is easily dissolved in alcohol.

I woke up the second morning in a cell at the Maniwaki police station with a black eye and a few good bruises. The moment I came to, it hit me like a ton of bricks: the explosion, little Josée, the guy with the beard crushed for a few grams of coke, the woman in the wheelchair, all those lives cut short – and me, still alive. More or less. I was thirsty. I was shaking. I was like a drowning person struggling to get to the surface to breathe. Except my air was a golden liquid. Binges have a life of their own: a few days, a few weeks, sometimes a few years. How long they last depends on several things: How long the body can take it. How much money you've got to burn. But most of all, how much pain you need to numb, how much rage you need to stifle, how much emptiness inside needs to be filled. I still had plenty of all that. It wasn't time to abandon ship yet.

It seems the Montreal police had been looking for me in connection with the death of the guy in the rubble. They took me back to the city in an unmarked police car with no door handles in the back. They dumped me in a cell at Montreal police headquarters and left me to cool my jets for a while. Then two detectives in suits questioned me. I told them everything I knew, though I didn't mention the Darling Tavern. After a while, they got bored. Me, too. They decided I wasn't the type to murder a guy twice my size with a six-foot beam. I had to promise to remain at their disposal for further questioning, then they cut me loose in the big city. I still had a hundred dollars in my pocket. I drank every penny of it.

A cyclist found me early the next morning in an advanced state of hypothermia. Somehow I'd ended up on a detour along the bicycle path on rue Notre-Dame, beside a factory wall across the street from the St. Lawrence Sugar refinery. He could easily have missed me: I had crawled into a heap of garbage and leaves to die. Or he could have seen me and just left me there. But he was a Good Samaritan. (Yes, they really exist.) I remember him well, a young man with an apple-green anorak and a pony-tail sticking out from under his helmet. He roused me gently from my stupor, rubbed my arms and shoulders, and tried to get me moving. Then he said:

– Hang in there, *monsieur*, I'm going for help.

I don't know why, but I remember his eyes. He had smiling eyes. And he wasn't fazed in the least, as if he rescued rubbies on the bicycle path every day. Maybe he did. He squeezed my shoulder before leaving. That I remember, too. Then I must have passed out again.

◆

– There he is! ... Gérard, where on earth have you been?!

That voice, that accent, the hospital corridor ...

There's a hell for drunks and I'm in it – that's what I thought when I opened my eyes. Everything else was a blur, but there was no mistaking Chantal: the little mocking eyes, the little turned up nose, the brownish-grey tweed suit, the little pearl necklace, the little Vuitton handbag, the faint fragrance of *Quelques Fleurs* by Houbigant. Oh, boy. There was a time in my life when I was a regular at Saint-Luc Hospital and, God knows why, but I'd given them Chantal's number to contact in an emergency. They must have had it on file.

– *Pauvre Gérard*. What happened?

For a moment I was sure I'd been transported back to 1969, the victim of a temporary tear in the warp and weft of the space-time continuum (as they say in science-fiction novels) ... Chantal and I were married ... she'd come to pick me up at the hospital one more time ... If I just hung on a while I'd be transported back to the present, with apologies from ground control on planet earth.

No such luck: it really was the present and it really was Chantal, thirty years older. As for me, I felt sixty years older. I tried moving. I must have moaned. I hurt all over, especially where I hang my hat. When I have a hat.

– Gérard, you're too old for this now, she cooed softly.

I never could resist a woman who takes pity on me. When they use that tone of voice, I crack. I guess I didn't get enough hugs when I was a kid.

– Oooooh, I answered.

The binge was over. It happens like that, when you least expect it. You go back to being a human being. The beast retreats to its cave. Mr. Hyde changes back to Dr. Jekyll.

Chantal took me to her place. She washed my clothes and made me chicken noodle soup. Why she has these outpourings of generosity towards me, I'll never know. I guess I should stop trying to understand and just be grateful. To keep her entertained I told her the whole story, right from the beginning: the explosion, my half-assed investigation, the Maniwaki Antler Festival (at least what I remembered of it). When I was finished, Chantal said:

– Every time you do these ridiculous things, Gérard, I remember why I married you.

Ah, the old game. I played along.

– Why's that, Chantal?

– Because you're impulsive, you're absolutely unpredictable. I never know what you're going to do next!

I smiled and waited for the punch line. It's like an old comedy sketch you've seen a dozen times and still love. She didn't keep me waiting.

– It's also why I left you.

That night I slept on the sofa. Everything was above board. While I was settling down for the night I heard Chantal locking the liquor cabinet. It wasn't necessary, but you never know. I called out to her:

– Chantal?

– What?

– You're terrific.

– I know.

– *Bonne nuit, Chantal.*

– *Bonne nuit, Gérard.*

◆

In the big city, AA never sleeps. There are meetings going on everywhere, at all hours of the day and night. It's reassuring, in a way, to know that the age-old story of the drunk is being recited again and again: "Hi, my name is Sophie, or Bruce, or Denis, or Sandra, and I'm an alcoholic." There's always someone, somewhere, saying: "I lived in hell and I haven't had a drink now in seven years, or six months, or three weeks." Yes, it's possible: you can choose not to drink. Some people actually do. That morning I found myself in a group downtown. They were mostly business types: hot-shot junior executives, lawyers with paunches, slick PR types, and a few pencil-pushers nearing retirement. *Mes frères,* all the same ... Someone should start Capitalists Anonymous: "Hi, my name is Tom and I've just laid off 500 employees. I couldn't help it. It's stronger than me." There should be steps for them, too: *We have acknowledged that we were powerless in the face of globalization and neo-liberalism, that we have lost control of our lives.* But would they make amends to the people they wronged? It doesn't matter. They were my enemies but they were my brothers, too, bosses and hatchet men alike, slaves of the bottle and slaves of profit. Whether they suffered less or were any less of a bastard than I am, I don't know. But I drank coffee with them and I told them my story. "My name is Gérard, and I've been sober for 24 hours."

After the meeting I went back to my place, across the street from my old childhood home, and I made a searching and fearless moral inventory of myself (Step

Four). I came to the conclusion that I lacked humility, that the Power greater than ourselves had sent me a Test I couldn't run away from, and that it was a waste of time looking for meaning in things I'd never understand. Acceptance, I told myself, acceptance. One day at a time, 24/7, 365. And then I got to Step Six: *to be entirely ready to have God remove all these defects of character.* That one I couldn't stomach.

– *Tabarnak!* I shouted. I don't want to change who I am. I just want to stop drinking!

Oh, oh. I was starting again, doing my mental pirouettes. If I kept on like this even AA would throw me out. Thoughts like that are dangerous, they lead straight to the nearest bar. I watched the kids playing ball hockey in the street. Then I skipped a step in my head. I went straight to Step Eight, made a list of all the people I had harmed, and agreed to make amends to them. Starting with Angéla. She must have been worried.

It was lunch-time. I sat at the counter. Angéla pretended she didn't see me. Rose, the owner, had to leave the stove to take my order. Angéla served me but didn't say a word. She was aloof and beautiful. I ate my hamburger steak and my raspberry upside-down cake. Then I drank three cups of coffee in a row. By the fourth cup, the Bien Bon was empty. It was two o'clock. Angéla sat down at the other end of the counter, lit a cigarette, and started reading the newspaper. I decided to jump in the deep end.

– Angéla, *je m'excuse.*

It wasn't much of an opening line, I have to admit. A few years back I had an Irish drinking buddy, a Frank O-something or other. He used to say:

– Catholicism is a great religion: you do whatever you want, you confess, the priest absolves you, and then you can start all over again. Let's drink to good old Jay Pee!

I guess he meant John Paul the Second. Me, I'm Catholic to the bone, a genius at every kind of excuse, lie, and honourable amend. Forgive me and I start again. Just ask my three exes.

– Angéla, I'm sorry.

She didn't move. It occurred to me that I didn't really owe her anything. We were just neighbours. We'd only eaten together a couple of times. But sharing life stories, especially stories like ours, creates bonds. And even if the bonds weren't very strong, there was always hope. So I started telling her what I had found out and what had happened to me over the past few days. At first there was no indication that she was even paying attention. But Rose came out of the kitchen, lit a cigarette, and started listening. After a while, Angéla raised her eyes from the newspaper and turned to look at me. When I finished my story, I said to her:

– You're right, Angéla. I stuck my nose in where it was none of my business and I hurt people. When you stir shit, it stinks. If you were worried about me, I apologize.

A mocking expression came over her face. She said:

– Worried? *Moi?* Not me. But people are looking for you. Your friend from the coroner's office called. They found your neighbour from the third floor.

I had a choice: I could lie or I could tell the truth. I lied. Not very well.

– I don't care anymore.

It didn't sound very convincing. I waited a few seconds, then added:

– Are you still angry?

Angéla looked at me and shook her head.

– It would probably be simpler if you call the coroner's office from here, Gérard. You can finish your coffee while you're talking to the guy.

And that's what I did.

The police had picked up Karl at the corner of Sainte-Catherine and Beaudry on the night of the explosion. He was stark naked, delirious, and high as a kite. That's nothing unusual for the Village, but unfortunately for Karl the cops just happened to be driving by. They took him to Pinel, where they sedated him. It took three days to get a name out of him and another two for the police to connect him to rue Darling. Now they knew who the streaker was, that Madame Kovacs had seen. They'd also gotten an ID on the woman with no face. Her family had claimed the body. Her name was Eve Parenteau. She was a friend of Karl's. Apparently she'd been visiting him, but that part of the story was still vague: my source didn't have any more details. I phoned the Pinel and they told me Karl had been transferred to the psych ward at the Royal Vic.

I asked Angéla for another cup of coffee. When she put it down in front of me, I said:

– Angéla, I'm pig-headed. I'm the most pig-headed person in the world.

– Tell me about it.

– I've got to know how the story ends. You understand, don't you?

– *Non*. But I'm listening.

– If I don't find out, it'll haunt me for ages.

– You wouldn't want to lose any sleep over it.

Really, the woman was so understanding.

– Can I ask you a favour, Angéla?

– What?

– Come with me to the Royal Vic.

– Are you nuts?

– Probably. But if you're with me, there's less chance I'll do something stupid.

– Hmm. Sure. And a couple just happens to look

more respectable, so there's less chance of you getting thrown out.

She read me like an open book. I have to admit, I'm pretty transparent.

– Well, that's true, too, I said.

– Gérard, look, I'll go with you. But you owe me one.

– *Pas de problème*. I owe you one.

– Now please stop calling me "vous."

– OK. Sure. *Vous aussi*. Shall we go?

– We close at five.

◆

It was dusk by the time we got there. The grey stone buildings of the Royal Victoria hospital looked like the set for a vampire movie. Everything was perfect, right down to the wind tearing the leaves off the trees and flocks of crows with walk-on parts. It wasn't hard to imagine a mad professor inside, administering LSD to his human guinea pigs on a secret mission for the CIA. "Take this, my dear lady, you'll see, it will make you feel better ..." You could almost hear Dracula's blood-curdling laugh echoing through the corridors. Those corridors weren't much to look at, either, at least not the ones in the psychiatric ward. If you weren't depressed going in, the decor would soon finish you off. Not to mention the locked doors, the intercoms, and the peepholes. They don't let just anyone in there. And getting out is even harder. I speak from experience.

The duty nurse, a chubby red-head with a kind smile, seemed pleased to see us. Karl's mother, Madame Godin, had been down from Val d'Or to visit him, but she'd had to go back up north and Karl hadn't had any visitors since. I introduced myself as a friend and neighbour, a fellow victim of the explosion. I said I'd been worried when Karl disappeared and was relieved to have finally found him. We'd brought chocolates and magazines to make it look convincing.

– How is he? I asked.

– He's still heavily sedated, but we're gradually bringing him around, the nurse said.

I told a little white lie to keep her talking.

– I was worried about him. He seemed agitated those last few days before the explosion. He'd stopped going to work and was blasting his music at full volume. It wasn't like him.

When I want to, I can be a charming old fart. A priest would give me absolution without waiting for my confession. The nurse fell for it.

– That doesn't surprise me, she said. Karl stopped taking his lithium. He was completely psychotic when the police picked him up.

– Oh. I see.

She commiserated.

– That's what happens with manic-depressives. As long as they're taking lithium, they can lead a normal life. But some of them miss their highs and stop taking their meds. And then they end up here.

– May we see him?

– *Oui*. But not for long. Room 1708. Don't say anything to him about his friend, or the explosion. I'm not sure he realizes what happened.

A man completely walled up. That's what we found in room 1708. Not locked up, walled up, inside a tomb of suffering, chemically cut off from life and the rest of humanity. You couldn't help but feel his pain and misery: it was tangible, it filled the room. It was as if the world had lost all its colour and there was only a grey monotone left. His sadness was a black hole sucking in everything around it. I was afraid I'd fall in and disappear. Angéla sensed it and took my arm. And then I said a ridiculous thing:

– *Bonjour.*

He seemed minuscule, a small, brown-haired man curled up in a bed miles too big for him. It took him a good minute to turn over; he moved with glacial slowness. He didn't say a word. He just looked at us.

– I'm your neighbour ... from rue Darling.

I could see from his eyes that he recognized me. Eventually he spoke:

– There ... is ... no ... thing ... left.

He separated each syllable. His voice was as thick as syrup. The anti-depressants, obviously. He spoke again:

– There ... is ... no ... thing ... left.

I knew what he meant. But I wanted more.

– Do you remember the night you were arrested?

He averted his eyes, slowly. I realized I wasn't going to get anything out of him. For all I knew, his memory was a blank. I placed the chocolates and the magazines on his bedside table and was wondering how best to take my leave when he spoke again:

– I ... on ... ly ... wan ... ted ... to ... go ... to ... Por ... tu ... gal.

– *Pardon?* What did you say?

He averted his eyes again. Angéla stepped forward and tried to draw him out, but there was only silence. We exchanged glances and decided to leave. I was just about to close the door when I heard his voice:

– *Mon ... sieur.*

I went back to the bed and bent down, to hear him better.

– Li ... thi ... um ... stops ... you ... from ... read ... ing. I ... can't ... read.

All the suffering of the world was in that voice. But he couldn't drag up another word. He turned away slowly, and curled back up into a ball.

We didn't say much on the drive back. Angéla

let me use her phone to call Karl's mother in Val d'Or. She was pleased that someone was taking an interest in her son, and talked freely about him. He'd had his first episode of mania five years before. They'd had to evict him from Place des Arts during a concert by the MSO. Apparently Karl wanted to make an important public announcement and Charles Dutoit wasn't amused. Karl was diagnosed as manic-depressive and put on lithium. But the medication made it hard to concentrate and read. He dropped out of university. He'd been studying history. He was 22. He had to earn a living somehow so he got a job at Radio Shack. Karl's mother didn't think he knew about the explosion yet. She didn't find out herself until she went to rue Darling to pick up some things to take to him in hospital. As for Eve, Karl and her had been lovers and had made a trip up to Val d'Or a few years ago, but later separated. Madame Godin hadn't known they were seeing each other again.

I went out. It was dark. I dropped in to the *Maison de la culture* and read a book about manic-depression, until closing time. Then I walked the streets of the neighbourhood, trying to piece together Karl's story from what little I knew. I couldn't let it go. I imagined Karl working at Radio Shack. Lithium masked the dangerous excesses of his illness. He'd been living a normal life, but that got boring. I could relate to that. He began missing the highs. He got tired of the chemicals that fogged his brain and prevented him from reading. So he threw out his meds. At first, everything was fine. He came alive again. His confidence came back, ideas started percolating, he was determined to live life to the fullest. He started buying stuff – three TVs, CDs, books on every subject, little games and silly toys and tricks. He listened to music, he craved music: his spirit soared. He read, he scribbled poems on every scrap of paper he could find. On the day of the explosion, he was completely out of it. He phoned an airline and bought two tickets to Portugal, then called Eve. Everything was crystal clear: they'd leave together. Eve could tell from his voice that something was wrong. She asked him if he was taking his lithium. He hung up on her. He unplugged the phone, turned off the TVs, turned off the music, and switched off the electricity. He didn't need those artificial connections to the world. He was the world. Alone in the dark, he felt strong and invincible. He took off his clothes. There was a knock on the door; it was Eve. She was worried about him. She wanted to talk to him. He had to get out. For a moment he thought about leaving by the window and flying, but he opted for the roof instead. He went out the back door, climbed the fire-escape to the roof, and started running. He was tall, he was beautiful, nothing could stop him. Eve was still knocking when the building blew up.

I ended my wandering back at the ruins on rue Darling. I realized I'd never know for sure what had happened. All I knew was that innocent people had died and that the survivors owed their lives to chance: young Patrick, too stoned to return home; Karl, in the middle of a full psychotic meltdown. And me, because my shoelace had come undone. Fate doesn't always pick the best and the brightest to save. Fate is deaf and blind. Fate is stupid and unfair. Fate is an imbecile. Fate plays dumb jokes.

And in the end, we all die anyway.

I stood there rooted to the spot, looking at the rubble, trying to conjure them up one last time: Adrienne, the little old lady on the first floor; Denise and her little Josée; the lovers on the second floor; and Eve. All of them dead, for nothing, for no reason. A light went on in one of the parked cars. It was Lieutenant Geoffrion, in civvies, in his own car, putting the final touch on his report.

– *Bonsoir,* Lieutenant.

– *'Soir.*

– You're working late.

– *Ouan.*

– What's new?

– *Rien.*

You can't push the Boomer. You'll get absolutely nowhere if you try. I held my tongue and waited. After a minute he looked up from his papers and said:

– The demolition crew arrives tomorrow.

– What? You mean you found the cause?

– No. It means they're in a hurry to rebuild.

– Do you have an idea, at least?

– No.

– There's no cause?

– There's always a cause. But it takes time to find it. And right now, everyone's in just too goddamn much of a hurry. If you want the truth, you've got to take the time to find it.

– If I were a drinking man, Lieutenant, I'd drink to that.

– To what?

– To taking the time you need.

We listened to the rumble of the city. I pulled out a pack of cigarettes.

– Time for a smoke, Lieutenant?

– Time for a smoke.

It was over. I'd run the course. There was no more air in the balloon. I wasn't any wiser or any happier. I was like someone who wins a game of solitaire and says:

– Well, that's that.

And starts another game.
It's called life.

◆

My name is Gérard and I'm an alcoholic. I've been sober for two months and two days. I'm sitting in a motel room on Route 117, not far from Kouchibouguac in New Brunswick.

I guess I should tell you what happened after I smoked that cigarette with Lieutenant Geoffrion in front of the ruins of my old building on rue Darling. But I don't feel like it. Let's just say I knocked on Angéla's door and she let me in. I still don't know what it means or where it'll lead, but I'm going to take the time to find out. Sometimes life pitches you a fastball, right in the middle of the strike zone. You should never waste a good pitch.

Angéla came back to New Brunswick to visit her children in their foster home. She asked me to come along. When she left the motel room this morning, she asked me to wait for her, and to take care of her when she gets back.

Because it's not easy watching your kids call a couple of strangers mom and dad.

So, I'm waiting for her.

When she comes back, I'll take her in my arms.

Maybe. Or maybe I'll let her sit by herself for a while and look at the ocean. I'll play it by ear. But I'm going to take care of her. I'm going to take care of her.

And later, if we feel like it, we'll go for lobster.

If it's in season.

ACKNOWLEDGEMENTS

The translator gratefully acknowledges the assistance of Bernard Émond, the hospitality of The Baltic Centre for Writers and Translators, in Visby, Sweden, and the support of The Canada Council for the Arts.

ABOUT THE AUTHOR

Bernard Émond was born in Montreal in 1951. After studies in anthropology and a Master's thesis on ethnographic cinema, he worked in the Canadian Arctic as a television instructor for Inuit Broadcasting. During the 1990s he made documentary films, including *Ceux qui ont le pas léger meurent sans laisser de traces*, named Best Documentary of 1992 by the Quebec Association of Film Critics (AQCC). Émond's first two feature films, *La femme qui boit* (2001) and *20h17 rue Darling* (2003), were selected for the International Critics' Week at the Cannes film festival. His next three features form a trilogy exploring the theological virtues, faith, hope, and charity. *La neuvaine* (2005), *Contre toute espérance* (2007), and *La donation* (2009) received numerous awards internationally, and *La neuvaine* was named Best Quebec Film of the Decade by the AQCC. Émond's 2012 feature film, *Tout ce que tu possèdes,* revolves around translating the poems of Edward Stachura.

ABOUT THE TRANSLATOR

John Gilmore is a former Montreal journalist. He is the author of *Swinging in Paradise: The Story of Jazz in Montreal* and a poetic novel, *Head of a Man*.

ABOUT THE FILM

20h17 rue Darling, written and directed by Bernard Émond, was selected for the International Critics Week at the 2003 Cannes Film Festival and named one of Canada's Top Ten Films for 2003 by the Toronto International Film Festival Group. In the same year the film won Best Male Actor (for Luc Picard in the role of Gérard) at the Festival international du film francophone de Namur, in Belgium, and the Audience Choice award as Best Canadian Feature Film at the Festival international du cinéma francophone en Acadie, in Moncton. The music soundtrack by Robert Marcel Lepage is available on the Ambiances Magnéthiques label.

ALSO BY BERNARD ÉMOND

<u>Books:</u>
Il y a trop d'images: Textes épars 1993-2010
*La perte et le lien: Entretiens sur le cinéma, la culture,
la société* (with Simon Galiero)
La quête spirituelle: Avec ou sans Dieu (with Rose
Dufour and Gilles Lussier)
Aani la bavarde

<u>Screenplays with Commentaries:</u>
Tout ce que tu possèdes: Scénario et regards croisés
La donation: Scénario et regards croisés
Contre toute espérance: Scénario et regards croisés
La neuvaine: Scénario et regards croisés

<u>Feature Films:</u>
Tout ce que tu possèdes (2012)
La donation (2009)
Contre toute espérance (2007)
La neuvaine (2005)
20h17 rue Darling (2003)
La femme qui boit (2001)

<u>Selected Documentary Films:</u>
Le temps et le lieu (2000)
L'épreuve du feu (1997)
La terre des autres (1995)
L'instant et la patience (1994)
Ceux qui ont le pas léger meurent sans laisser de traces
(1992)

TRANSLATOR'S NOTES

Page 2. *Les Rougon-Macquart*: A cycle of 20 novels by Émile Zola which follow several generations of a fictional French family during the 19th century. Pléiade editions, published by Gallimard, are high-quality, critical editions of major works of French and world literature, leather-bound and printed on Bible paper.

Page 6. *Liberté*: A quarterly revue of arts and politics, published in Montreal.

Page 8. **immigrant investor:** Foreign business people with money to invest are fast-tracked for immigration and citizenship in Canada.

Page 8. **October Crisis**: In late 1970, civil liberties were suspended and the Canadian army deployed in Quebec following the kidnapping of a British diplomat and a Quebec cabinet minister by members of the Front de Libération du Québec (FLQ). More than 450 people including artists and intellectuals were detained without charge. The Quebec minister was killed; the British diplomat eventually released.

Page 9. **Antoine Doinel:** A recurring character in five films by François Truffaut, often regarded as Truffault's alter ego.

Page 14. **the first floor:** In Montreal, the first floor is usually the ground floor. Some first floor apartments are a few steps above ground and have low balconies.

Page 14. **Act of God**: In English in the original text.

Page 14. **Sun Youth**: A Montreal community service organization which helps victims of house fires and other disasters.

Page 19. **Hautes études commerciales:** Canada's oldest business school, now officially called HEC Montréal.

Page 20. **Angus rail shops**: A large railcar manufacturing and repair facility, closed in 1992.

Page 21. **Amen and Praise the Lord**: In English in the original text.

Page 21. **Little Burgundy:** A neighbourhood in south-central Montreal, the historic home of the city's English-speaking, working-class black community.

Page 22. **Boom Boom ... the Canadiens**: Bernie Geoffrion was a legendary Montreal hockey player, nick-named "Boom Boom" for his powerful slapshot. The Canadiens is the name of Montreal's professional hockey team. (See also *habitant*, below.)

Page 25. **Glaneuses**: A Montreal charity selling used clothing and furniture.

Page 30. **I climbed the stairs**: In Montreal's older, three-floor residential buildings, the stairs to the second floor are often outside. From there an enclosed inner stairwell leads to the third floor.

Page 30. ***Pot-Bouille:*** One of the novels in Zola's *Les Rougon-Macquart*. Others mentioned later are *L'Assommoir, Germinal,* and *Nana.*

Page 36. **National Bank:** Quebec's largest bank, with headquarters in Montreal.

Page 47. **Young Catholic Workers:** Jeunesse Ouvrière Catholique, an international lay organization of the Catholic church which promotes workers' rights and social justice. The Quebec branch started in 1932 but lost influence during the 1960s with the rise of trade unions.

Page 48. **Order of the Holy Sacrament**: A fictitious order invented by the author.

Page 49. **Magnétothèque:** A Quebec organization producing audio books for the visually impaired, now called Vues et Voix.

Page 49. *Trente Arpents*: A Quebec novel first published in Paris in 1938. Ringuet was the nom-de-plume of author Philippe Panneton. The novel won prizes in France and Quebec, and Felix and Dorothea Walter's translation, *Thirty Acres*, won Canada's Governor General's Award in 1940. The excerpt here is from the Walter's translation in the New Canadian Library Edition published by McClelland & Stewart, 2009, 46. *Arpent* is a French unit of measure approximately equal to an acre.

Page 49. *Maison de la culture*: Montreal's neighbourhood arts and cultural centres. Some contain branches of the city library.

Page 49. *habitant*: A Quebec small-hold farmer, often poor. The word is sometimes used pejoratively to mean a country bumpkin, but is also the affectionate nickname (shortened to "Habs" in

English) of the Canadiens hockey team, many of whose early players were from rural Quebec.

Page 50. *Un Canadien errant*: A Quebec folk song written by Antoine Gérin-Lajoie after the failed Lower Canada rebellion of 1837–38; those rebels not killed were forced into exile. The song became a popular tribute to the hundreds of thousands of Quebec farmers and unemployed workers who migrated to the USA in search of jobs during the 19th and early 20th centuries.

Page 52. *petit-Canada*: Communities of French-Canadian emigrants in the United States, particularly in New England. (See *Un Canadien errant,* above.)

Page 54. *madeleines*: Small sponge cakes from the Lorraine region of France. Marcel Proust, in *À la recherche du temps perdu (In Search of Lost Time),* used *madeleines* to show how a taste could trigger involuntary memories.

Page 54. *dépanneur*: A neighbourhood convenience store selling beer, wine, tobacco, and basic groceries.

Page 55. **Educ'alcool**: A not-for-profit organization promoting responsible drinking.

Page 58. **home**: In English in the original text.

Page 59. **CEGEP**: Quebec's post-secondary public colleges. The acronym, for Collège d'enseignement général et professionnel, is used in English as well.

Page 63. **whatever the hell that means**: In English in the original text, as "whatever that means."

Page 67. **Caisse Populaire**: Quebec's network of cooperatively-owned credit unions.

Page 68. *mes semblables, mes frères*: Literally "my fellow men, my brothers." A variation on —*Hypocrite lecteur,—mon semblable,—mon frère!*, the last line of Baudelaire's opening poem in *Les Fleurs du Mal* (1857).

Page 74. **Beaver Lake**: A small, man-made lake atop Mount Royal.

Page 76. **Acadian peninsula**: In the northeastern corner of New Brunswick, so-called for its French-speaking Acadian population.

Page 82. **toonie**: Canada's two dollar coin.

Page 86. **Chic Resto Pop**: A community restaurant in the Hochelaga-Maisonneuve district serving inexpensive meals while providing job training for unemployed workers.

Page 89. **E.B. Eddy**: Founder of the E.B. Eddy Company, a Quebec manufacturer of wooden matches.

Page 90. **Laprairie**: A suburb of Montreal on the south-shore of the St. Lawrence River.

Page 91. **Big deal**: In English in the original text.

Page 91. **Yes Master …:** In English in the original text, but as: "Yes Master. As you please Master. Only water for me, Master."

Page 93. **SAQ:** Quebec's liquor stores, run by the Société des alcools du Québec. In English, people sometimes refer to the stores as "the sack."

Page 93. **"Moderation is always in good taste":** *La modération a bien meilleur goût,* a slogan used by Éduc'alcool (see above).

Page 95. **Porte-du-Nord:** A tourist information and service centre 40 kilometres north of Montreal, considered the gateway to the Laurentian mountains.

Page 95. **Perly's:** A Canadian publisher of road maps.

Page 95. **Sainte-Rose:** A district in the city of Laval, adjacent to Montreal.

Page 103. **Oh, boy:** In English in the original text.

Page 109. **the Village:** Also known as the Gay Village, an inner-city neighbourhood and nightlife district popular with the city's gay and lesbian community.

Page 109. **Pinel:** The Institut Philippe-Pinel de Montréal, a hospital specializing in forensic psychiatry and the assessment and treatment of violent patients.

Page 110. **Royal Vic:** The Royal Victoria Hospital, on the southern slope of Mount Royal.

Page 111. **mad professor ... the CIA**: During the 1950s and 1960s, the psychiatric wing of the Royal Victoria Hospital was one of many sites of a secret CIA research program aimed at developing mind control and psychological torture techniques. Under the guidance of Donald Ewen Cameron, then chairman of the World Psychiatric Association and president of the Canadian Psychiatric Association, unsuspecting patients at the Royal Vic were given LSD, paralytic drugs, and high doses of electroconvulsive therapy. Some were kept in drug-induced comas for weeks and subjected to endless noise. Many were left permanently damaged. It wasn't until the 1980s that journalists uncovered the full extent of the Canadian program and discovered that the Canadian government had helped fund it.

Page 115. **MSO**: Montreal Symphony Orchestra, conducted by Charles Dutoit from 1977 to 2002.

Page 119. **Kouchibouguac**: A town and nearby national park on the shore of the Gulf of St. Lawrence, in eastern New Brunswick.

Printed in February 2014
by Gauvin Press,
Gatineau, Québec